F
SL

86-79

# OMEGA STATION

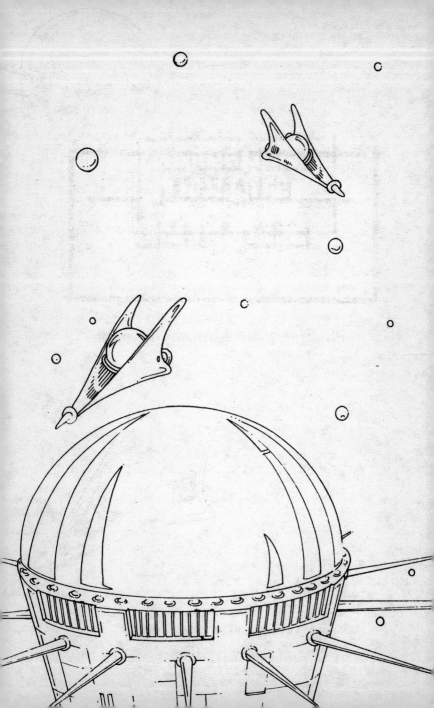

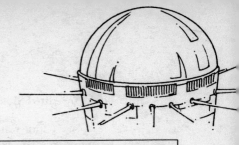

# OMEGA STATION
## by Alfred Slote

### illustrated by Anthony Kramer

A Harper Trophy Book
**HARPER & ROW, PUBLISHERS**

Other books by Alfred Slote available in Trophy

Clone Catcher

Hang Tough, Paul Mather

Matt Gargan's Boy

My Robot Buddy

My Trip to Alpha I

Rabbit Ears

Omega Station
Text copyright © 1983 by Alfred Slote
Illustrations copyright © 1983 by Anthony Kramer
Printed in the United States of America. For information address Harper & Row, Junior Books, 10 East 53rd Street, New York, N.Y. 10022. Published simultaneously in Canada by Fitzhenry & Whiteside Limited, Toronto.

Library of Congress Cataloging in Publication Data
Slote, Alfred.

Omega Station
Summary: Jack Jameson and his robot twin, Danny One, must save the universe from a mad scientist.
  [1. Science fiction.  2. Outer space—Fiction.
3. Robots—Fiction]  I. Kramer, Anthony, ill.  II. Title.
PZ7.S635Om  1983    [E]    82-48461
ISBN 0-397-32035-3
ISBN 0-397-32036-1 (lib. bdg.)  85-45395

"A Harper Trophy book"
ISBN 0-06-440167-7 (pbk.)

Designed by Al Cetta
First Harper Trophy edition, 1986.
Published in hardcover by J.B. Lippincott, New York.

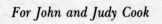

*For John and Judy Cook*

# Contents

# OMEGA STATION

# 1 Start of an Adventure

Hay fever pills? I believe in them. They saved my life and Danny's life, too, and the life of the whole world, for that matter.

But that's the end of my story, and Danny One Jameson—my robot buddy and brother—says that the way to tell a story is to start at the beginning.

The beginning consists of me and my backpack getting out of the school air bus at the corner of Church and Dexter roads in Region III, U.S.A., where we live.

Danny was sitting under an apple tree waiting for me. Because he's a robot, Danny doesn't have to go to school. He just gets programmed by Dr. Atkins once a year to keep up with me. And in some cases (like arithmetic) to stay ahead of me. Which isn't too hard to do.

Anyway, just as I was stepping off the escalator from the school air bus, the little radio in Danny's belly button went off.

"Beep, beep," his belly button chirped, "beep, beep."

The kids on the air bus heard it. They laughed and waved. They knew all about Danny. In fact, once Danny pretended to be me and went to school in my place. But the teacher suspected something was wrong because Danny knew all the answers.

We can manage switches like that because Danny and I look exactly alike. Danny's designed to look and talk just like me. We're practically identical twins, with just a couple of differences. Danny walks stiff-in-the-knee, like all robots. (Although when I imitate him and walk stiff-in-the-knee, then that's really not a difference.)

Secondly, I don't have a radio behind my belly button, which is probably a good thing for me—a human being.

"Someone's calling you," I said.

"I know," Danny said. "I can hear it. I just don't want to answer it."

"Why not?"

"I bet it's trouble."

I laughed. "I bet it's the start of another adventure."

We were both really saying the same thing. For

[4]

me, troubles are adventures. For Danny, adventures are troubles.

Once I asked Dr. Atkins why he had programmed Danny to be so cautious.

"Because you're not," Dr. Atkins said. "It wouldn't have done you any good to give you a robot buddy as reckless as you. This way you make a good team."

And we have. Together we once fooled a robot-napper and together we once saved a colony of robot boys and girls on C.O.L.A.R.

Dr. Atkins said after our C.O.L.A.R. adventure that he was going to call on us to help him if he ever had any more troubles. Which was why Danny didn't want to answer the call on his belly-button radio.

But finally he pushed in his belly button, and sure enough, Dr. Atkins's familiar voice floated out.

"Danny One Jameson. This is Leopold Atkins. Can you hear me?"

"Yes, sir," Danny said loudly, giving me a 'what did I tell you' look.

"Is Jack with you?"

"Yes, sir. He's here. He just got off his school air bus."

"Can he hear me?"

I bent down and talked into Danny's belly button. "Yes, sir. I hear you fine."

I was glad no one was around watching me talk into Danny's belly button.

"All right," Dr. Atkins said crisply, "both of you—pay attention! I've talked to your parents. They know that I need your help. And that I need it right away. Where are you?"

"At the corner of Church and Dexter in Region III," said Danny.

"Stay there!" Dr. Atkins commanded. "I'll have an air cruiser over there in five minutes. It will bring you to the factory."

Click. He switched off. No good-bye. No asking us if we wanted to be fetched by his air cruiser. But that was Dr. Atkins for you. A genius. Inventor of the Atkins robots that look more human than human beings.

Danny looked gloomy. "I was hoping we could play basketball in the driveway this afternoon."

"We can play when we get back from his office," I said.

"I bet we don't."

"Why do you say that?"

"Because this sounds serious. He spoke to our folks. He wants to see us both. The only reason he ever wants us both is because we look alike and you can imitate my robot walk perfectly. You know what that means?"

"Adventures!" I said.

"Troubles!" Danny said.

We could have argued that a long time, but just then Dr. Atkins's air cruiser zoomed overhead, circled, and then let down its escalator.

Up we went, and a few minutes later we were in Dr. Atkins's office in the heart of the Atkins Robot Factory.

## 2 The Most Dangerous Man in the Universe

The Atkins Robot Factory is an immense building. Plastic, rubber, steel, copper, chemicals, insulation all come in at one end . . . and robots come out the other.

Of course, there's more to it than that. There's computer programming and electronics and design and mathematics. And at the center of it all is Dr. Leopold Atkins.

Dr. Atkins is a tall, gray-haired man with stern blue eyes. Sometimes I think he looks like an iceberg. Other times he just looks like God. Either way he's pretty impressive.

He was sitting behind his huge desk when we came in. He looked grim.

"Sit down, both of you," he said. "I want to thank you for coming."

Danny and I glanced at each other. Dr. Atkins never thanked anyone for anything. So he really had to be worried about something.

"I can see you're wondering what this is all about," he said.

"Yes, sir," we said.

"Well, so am I," he said.

Wow, I thought. If he didn't know why he'd sent for us, then we'd never know either.

But, of course, it was just Dr. Atkins's exaggerated way of speaking.

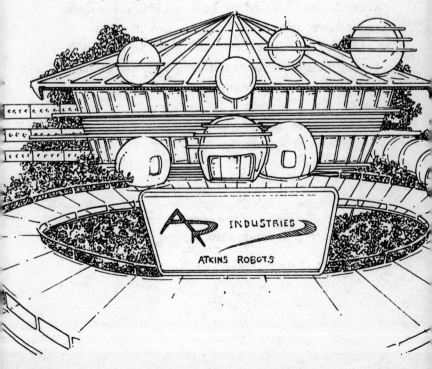

He rose to his feet and looked down at us grimly.

"We have troubles," he said. "The whole world has troubles. The universe will have troubles."

"Nothing new about that, is there?" I said and felt Danny wince. He wished I wouldn't pipe up like that.

"There is something new about this kind of trouble, Jack," Dr. Atkins said. He began pushing buttons on a computer console next to his desk.

"I am going to have the art computer draw you a picture of the most dangerous man in the universe. It will be based on the data I kept on him plus projections as to what he must look like now."

I didn't quite get the meaning of all that, but the computer did because on the big Vue/Screen hanging down from the ceiling some lines began to appear.

At first they were fuzzy and looked like this:

After a few seconds they looked like this:

And finally all the lines swam into focus and looked like this:

The computer clicked off.

"Hmmm . . ." said Dr. Atkins. "So that's what Otto looks like now."

"Otto?" I asked.

"Yes. Otto Drago," Dr. Atkins said, "a vicious, unprincipled, brilliant scientist who once worked for me."

"He doesn't look so dangerous, Dr. Atkins," I said. "In fact, he looks downright funny. He's got big ears and pop eyes. He sort of looks like a clown."

"A clown who kills!" Dr. Atkins snapped. "It's because he *looks* so harmless and jovial that he *is* so dangerous. Behind that false happy face lies a brain totally committed to evil. A foul heart. A mean spirit. I know this because at one time Otto Drago was my right-hand assistant. He helped me design the first true Atkins robot."

"One of your ancestors," I said to Danny.

"Funny," Danny said. He looked more worried than ever.

"What's this Drago guy done?" I asked. "And where is he?"

"Where he is I don't know," said Dr. Atkins. "But what he's doing I can show you right now."

Dr. Atkins pushed a button on his Vue/Phone. Instantly the picture on the Vue/Screen changed, and now we were looking into a large white room. It looked like a hospital operating room.

In the center of the room, under a bright light, a small group of people were huddled over someone lying on a table. They had tools in their hands.

"Pliers," one of them said. And another handed him a pair of pliers.

"Soldering iron," he now ordered.

He was handed a soldering iron.

It was clear to Danny and me that the people—or robots—on the screen were repairing a damaged Atkins robot.

"The facts are these," said Dr. Atkins. "For some unknown reason, my former assistant Otto Drago has been robotnapping Atkins robots and then destroying them wire by wire, transistor by transistor, silicon chip by silicon chip. You are looking at a robot who has managed to escape from Drago's clutches. We are working hard to save this robot right now."

Dr. Atkins pushed the SPEAK button on his Vue/Phone.

We heard his voice break in on the hushed tones of the Emergency Repair Operating Room.

"Simmons, how is our patient doing?" Dr. Atkins asked.

One of the people—or robots—in white coats turned away from the operating table to face us. "We are rewiring the voice box now, Doctor. We should know soon."

"Let me know the moment you're done. I've got Jack and Danny Jameson here now. I want them to hear his story firsthand."

"Yes, sir."

Dr. Atkins switched off the Vue/Phone. The operating repair room vanished from the screen.

"That robot's name is Bob Three. He is a citizen of C.O.L.A.R. A planet both of you are very familiar with."

"Yes, sir," we said.

"A week ago Bob Three disappeared from the surface of C.O.L.A.R. Before that several other Atkins robots disappeared from the surface of C.O.L.A.R. Bob Three is the first one we have recovered."

"Where was he recovered?" Danny asked Dr. Atkins.

"In outer space. There is a holographic record of the recovery taken by the spaceship that found him. Would you like to see it?"

"Yes, sir," I said.

Danny was silent. We were getting in deeper and deeper every moment. We both knew that.

"It's not pleasant to look at," Dr. Atkins warned us.

Danny nodded. "I'd like to see it too, Dr. Atkins," he said.

"Good."

Dr. Atkins pushed some more buttons, and now the Vue/Screen lighted up with a completely different picture. A three-dimensional picture. We were now on board a spaceship . . . looking through the flight control window at the darkness of outer space.

A laser light beam cut through the darkness.

"This is the holographic record of Shuttle Flight 23A going from M Colony to J Colony," Dr. Atkins said. "We pick up the flight as it begins to cross the Earth–Moon industrial highway."

The Earth–Moon highway was probably the busiest spaceway in the universe. Soon, through the flight windows, we could see all kinds of space vehicles

[ 14 ]

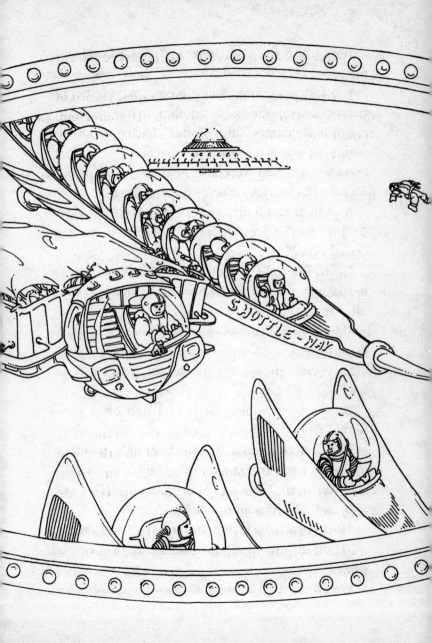

lighted up in the laser beams. Big ships and little ones, space trucks carrying raw materials to the moon for processing, space buses carrying people from one space colony to another. Space taxis, special interplanetary ships under charter to athletic teams—it was a busy part of space.

As we watched we could hear the two pilots of Shuttle Flight 23A talking to each other.

And then suddenly one of them said:

"Jim, there's an unidentified object off the starboard bow."

Off to the right we could see something floating in space. A piece of trash? Something that had fallen off a spaceship?

"Good Lord," the pilot named Jim said, "I think it's a person . . ."

Sure enough, we too could see a head, arms, legs . . .

"Some poor soul must have fallen off a moon flight."

The body, illuminated in the laser light, was floating on its back, its arms hanging limply by its sides.

"Poor devil," the first pilot said. "Well, let's net him and take him along with us."

"Ready to launch the landing net," Jim said.

"Hold it!" the first pilot exclaimed. "Do you see what I see?"

We all saw it. The dead body—it had to be dead

because no human being can live for two seconds in airless outer space—this *dead* body was actually waving an arm, feebly, in the direction of the shuttle flight, beckoning for help.

"It can't be a human being," Jim said. "It has to be a robot."

"And by the human look of it, an Atkins robot," the first pilot added.

At the mention of his name, Dr. Atkins nodded approvingly. Atkins robots looked more like people than people did.

"But what the devil is an Atkins robot doing floating in outer space?" Jim wanted to know.

"That's what I want to know too," Dr. Atkins said.

"We'll soon find out," said the first pilot. "Launch landing net!"

"Net away!"

A steel net shot out from the side of the shuttle flight, like ink from a giant squid, and settled gently down over the floating robot.

"Good work, Jim. Bring him in easy."

Slowly the landing net returned to the ship with the Atkins robot inside it, swaying back and forth in the netting, like a trapped fish.

As the net got closer we got a good look at the robot's face. It was horrible. His face was scarred and cracked and scorched.

I looked away.

"Good Lord," said the first pilot, "what has that robot been through?"

Dr. Atkins pushed a button. The holographic flight record was turned off.

"That's all there is," he said to us. "When they brought Bob Three in last night, he could only whisper one word to us: 'Drago.' "

Dr. Atkins looked at us.

"There is only one Drago who works with robots. Otto Drago. I fired him because I soon learned that his only interest in the science of robotics was to create robots for evil purposes. And now he turns up again—a name in the mouth of a very sick robot. We . . ."

He stopped. A red light started blinking on his Vue/Phone. Simmons's face appeared on the screen.

"Yes, Simmons?" Dr. Atkins said.

"Bob Three is in the Recovery Room now, sir. He cannot talk much but . . ."

"We're on our way," said Dr. Atkins.

# 3  The Dying Robot

The way to the Recovery Room led past the Programming Department (where they program behavior for Atkins robots), past the Physiognomy Department (where they design human faces for Atkins robots), past the Personality Department (where they work out the mathematics of cheerfulness, grumpiness—whatever you want your robot to be like), past the assembly lines on which Danny was built two years ago, past the Repair Department with its emergency operating room, and finally to a door that had a sign on it saying:

QUIET PLEASE

robot recovery room

We went in.

It was a small room with a metal bed in the middle. Surrounding the bed was an array of electronic devices: oscilloscopes, battery recharge machines, dynamometers, spectrum analyzers. Many wires led into and out of the robot named Bob Three as he lay there on the bed.

Fans blew cool air across his plastic skin. They were trying to cool the welds made by the repair team. It looked like every inch of Bob Three's body was cracked.

His eyes were open, staring at nothing.

By the poor robot's side stood Simmons, the repair specialist: tall, thin, and worried.

Dr. Atkins strode purposefully across the room and right up to Bob Three's bed. He looked down grimly at Bob Three.

"Will he be able to hear me, Simmons?"

"Yes, sir," replied Simmons. "He can hear. And he can talk. But I would not let him talk too long, sir. The welds might give way, and then we will lose him completely."

"That's a chance we'll have to take," Dr. Atkins said, curtly. "More is at stake here than Bob Three's life."

A good philosophy, I thought, provided you were not Bob Three.

Dr. Atkins leaned over Bob Three.

"Bob Three! This is Dr. Leopold Atkins speaking. Can you hear me?"

The almost lifeless eyes of the robot turned toward Dr. Atkins. You could tell he heard.

"I know that you are in pain right now, Bob Three. But it is my firm intention to fix you up as good as new and send you home to C.O.L.A.R."

A look of alarm flickered in Bob Three's eyes.

"What's the matter? Don't you want to go back to C.O.L.A.R.?"

Bob Three's lips twisted; you could tell that it would hurt him to talk. The word clawed out painfully from his newly repaired voice box: "No . . ."

"What are you afraid of on C.O.L.A.R.?"

The robot's lips twisted again. The word came out almost in agony: "Drago . . ." he whispered.

"Otto Drago doesn't live on C.O.L.A.R. Or"—Dr. Atkins frowned—"does he?"

Bob Three closed his eyes. Metal fatigue was setting in.

"Perhaps we're rushing things, sir," said Simmons. "Some of his welds have not yet cooled."

The soft whirring of the fans seemed to support his statement.

"Unfortunately we can't wait," Dr. Atkins said. "Drago may be robotnapping more C.O.L.A.R. citizens right now. Bob Three, where did you meet Otto Drago?"

Bob Three opened his eyes and looked at Dr. Atkins. And then tears came into his eyes.

"The devil take me for programming emotion into robots," Dr. Atkins said, exasperated.

Danny and I looked at each other. One of us should talk to Bob Three. He was afraid of Dr. Atkins.

Danny should do it, I thought. He was a robot too. "Go ahead," I said to him.

"Can I talk to Bob Three, Dr. Atkins?" Danny asked.

"What makes you think he'll talk to you?"

"He might find it easier talking to a robot."

"I doubt it, but you can try. This is what I want to find out from him. Where did he meet Otto Drago? What did Drago do to him? Why did he do it? Why is he afraid to return to C.O.L.A.R.? What has happened to the other robot boys and girls missing from C.O.L.A.R.? And finally, how did he happen to be floating around in space when the shuttle picked him up?"

Danny shook his head. I knew he was thinking that that was an awful lot to ask from a very sick robot. Typical of Dr. Atkins though. A sort of inhuman human.

"I'll try," Danny said. He leaned over the bed. "Bob Three," he said, "I'm Danny One Jameson."

"I remember you," Bob Three whispered. "You

and your human brother, Jack, came to C.O.L.A.R."

"That's right. And we want to help again. What happened to you, Bob?"

Bob Three was silent.

"Something happened to you on the surface of C.O.L.A.R., didn't it?"

"Yes," he whispered.

"Tell us about it."

But he was silent once more. It hurt him to talk. Each of us could see that.

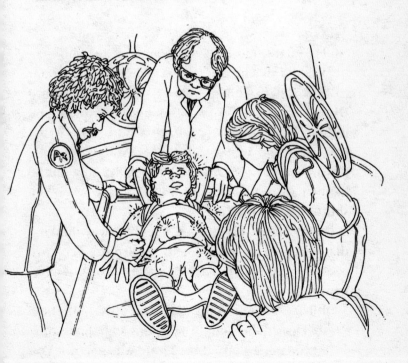

Finally Simmons, the repair specialist, broke the silence: "He knows that if he talks, his welds will break, and we won't be able to save him."

Bob Three nodded. That's right, his eyes were saying to us. If I talk, I might save the others, but I know that I will self-destruct.

He hesitated.

And then he talked.

# 4  Bob Three's Tale

It was a warm morning on the surface of C.O.L.A.R. Jeff, the leader of C.O.L.A.R., had assigned tasks to most of the robot boys and girls.

But they were all happy tasks: laying out baseball diamonds, stocking the trout ponds with baby fish, planting trees and bushes.

C.O.L.A.R. was becoming a planet of great beauty. Once the Atkins robots who lived there had all lived underground. But not now.

Jeff reminded all the robot boys and girls going out to their chores that they had to return to C.O.L.A.R. City for battery charges during the day; a remote charging system had not yet set up.

Ann Two and Carl Three, Jeff's assistants, were monitoring the battery charges that day.

"My job," Bob Three whispered to us, "was to

look for places that could be used for soccer fields. Jeff told me that when I was done with that I could go fishing. I love to fish."

Bob Three soon found two good flat fields and noted their locations on the map. Then he got out his fishing rod and headed for a small trout pond that had been stocked the previous year.

The pond was past a meadow and just beyond a little hill. It was a pretty pond. Bob Three fished for a while without catching anything, and then he lay down and watched the clouds drift over C.O.L.A.R. One cloud looked like a turtle, he thought. Another looked like a castle with huge twin turrets. And then between the two turrets, Bob Three saw a tiny black dot appear.

It got larger and larger.

"I realized then," whispered Bob Three, "that it wasn't part of the cloud. It was a spaceship coming toward C.O.L.A.R. A strange ship with black and red markings.

"I thought it was heading right for me. Which was crazy. We have a spaceport at C.O.L.A.R. City. There was nothing where I was except the pond, a meadow, and the little hill."

The strange spaceship circled the pond and then fired its retro-rockets for a landing on the shore of the pond. Its stabilizer legs came down, and like a spider it settled onto the land. Bob Three got to his feet. He was curious. He wasn't scared. Although he should have been.

(Here Bob Three paused in his tale while repair specialist Simmons examined the welds on his body. The cooling fans kept blowing. Bob Three rested a moment longer and then resumed his tale.)

"The ship's landing ramp came out and the door opened. I almost fainted. Out onto the ramp came two of our friends from C.O.L.A.R. who had been missing for over a week: Ted Eight and Sally Five.

" 'Ted! Sally!' I shouted. 'Where have you two been?'

"They laughed. 'Hello, Bob Three,' Ted said. 'I see you're goofing off as usual.'

" 'He's not goofing off,' Sally said. 'He's fishing.'

" 'Same thing as far as Jeff is concerned,' Ted said.

"The two of them came down the landing ramp and walked over to me. They looked fine, I thought. But I scolded them just the same.

" 'You two should be ashamed of yourselves. We've been worried sick about you. We've been looking all over for you. Jeff even went back into the tunnels to see if you'd gone down there and got lost.'

"Sally laughed. 'You shouldn't have been worrying about us, Bob Three,' she said. 'We've been having a wonderful time. And so have Barbara Two and Sam Ten.'

" 'Where are they? And where've you been? And where did you get that spaceship?' I asked them.

"Ted said: 'We live on Omega Station now, Bob. And it's the best place in the universe to live.'

" 'Omega Station? Where's that?'

" 'Not far from here. Want to come back with us?' Sally asked.

" 'No, I don't. Jeff will want to see you both.'

"Sally giggled. 'We don't want to see Jeff. We don't live on C.O.L.A.R. anymore. We don't take orders from Jeff or anyone. On Omega Station we have fun all day long, and we don't need battery charges either.' "

(Here Dr. Atkins, standing by our side, grunted that such a thing was impossible. Atkins robots had to have battery charges.)

"That's what I thought too, Dr. Atkins," Bob Three whispered to him. "And that's what I said to them. They said: 'Come see for yourself, Bob Three. And if you don't like life on Omega Station, then we'll bring you right back.' "

Bob Three closed his eyes. The effort of speaking had exhausted him. He rested a moment. Simmons looked worriedly at the welds on his body. You could tell he didn't think they'd hold up.

"They lied to me," Bob Three whispered. "Though maybe they couldn't help it. I went with them. Into their spaceship. And we went to Omega Station . . ."

He fell silent again.

Dr. Atkins leaned forward. "Where was this Omega Station, Bob Three?"

Bob Three looked at him and then winced. We heard a "pfft" sound somewhere on his body. A weld had just broken.

"Sir," Simmons pleaded with Dr. Atkins, "I think he should rest."

"Where was Omega Station? Speak up! For the sake of every other robot on C.O.L.A.R."

Bob Three looked at him and then at all of us. His voice was a pain-racked whisper. "I don't know. It wasn't far. It wasn't near. By the time we got there, I needed a battery charge. Ted recharged me. 'I thought you said I wouldn't need charges on Omega Station,' I told Ted.

" 'Oh,' Ted said, 'that's only after Doctor Drago redesigns you. You're going to meet him now.'

" 'Doctor Drago's twice as smart as Dr. Atkins,' Sally said."

There was another "pfft" sound from Bob Three's body. A weld popped on the upper part of his right arm.

"I beg of you, sir," Simmons pleaded with Dr. Atkins.

"And did you meet Otto Drago?" Dr. Atkins asked, ignoring Simmons.

"Yes, sir. I . . . I . . . went into a small house . . ." Bob Three's voice was faint now. "Into a room. With mirrors. He . . . took my arm. He said I'd be . . . happy. I'd soon see Barbara Two and Sam Ten. He was . . . friendly. He told me not to . . . worry. He put wires on my wrists. Onto my chest. And then . . ."

Bob Three's voice broke. He couldn't go on.

"Stick with it, lad!" Dr. Atkins urged. "And then what?"

Bob Three swallowed. We all leaned forward to hear his next words.

". . . and then I went down . . . down . . . It was blue . . . wet . . . there was pain."

He looked at us and suddenly his eyes were clear. "The pain was terrible," he said clearly and loudly.

And with that last burst the welds began popping everywhere on his body. "Pfft" . . . "pfft" . . . "pfft" . . .

Dr. Atkins paid no attention. "And then what, lad? And then what?"

"Then the net came out. And the spaceship found me," Bob Three said. Those were his last words.

His eyes closed.

The only sounds now were the rest of the welds popping and the wires and silicon chips ceasing their functioning inside his body with little dead clinking sounds.

In front of our eyes, his whole body began coming apart now: fracturing, splitting, disintegrating.

I looked away. So did Danny.

Simmons wept openly.

Only Dr. Atkins appeared unmoved. He stared grimly down at the young robot who had just stopped functioning. And then he said softly:

"You were a brave young robot, Bob Three. I will build another Bob Three, and we will design him to look exactly like you, and we will name him Bob Three, and we will program him to be as brave and as intelligent as you."

And that was as close to a funeral speech as Dr. Atkins would ever make.

He turned to us.

"Something blue . . . something wet . . . and something painful destroyed Bob Three," he said. "Pain has no color. Water can be blue. But when is water painful? When something passing through it destroys metal, plastic, and certainly could destroy flesh. What is that something passing through the water? And why does Drago expose a robot to it?"

It was fascinating to watch Dr. Atkins's mind at work.

"He's using Atkins robots to work on something that in the process destroys them. We must find out what it is and put a stop to it."

He looked at us again. "Will you two go to Omega Station for me?"

"What can we do?" I asked.

"Between a robot who looks like a human being and a human being who is the exact image of the robot and can imitate him perfectly, we can trap this evil man. Jack, open your mouth!"

That was about the last thing I expected Dr. Atkins to say then.

I opened my mouth in astonishment.

Dr. Atkins peered inside. "Hmmm . . . perfect! Your tooth formation is perfect. It will work."

"What will work?" Danny asked.

"Step One of my plan. But before we go any further, I must have the answer: are you both willing to undertake this dangerous mission?"

"I am," I said.

Danny didn't answer.

Dr. Atkins looked at the robot he had built as a birthday present for me two years ago. He had programmed caution into him, and now Danny was being cautious . . . with *him*. I grinned.

"Danny One Jameson," Dr. Atkins said, "I appeal to your instincts of robothood. It is possible that every Atkins robot in the universe might be destroyed by Otto Drago. Further, I suspect this dreadful man is probably using robots to create something that will destroy the world as we know it today. Within the blue . . . the wet . . . and the pain, something monstrous is being built. Will you go to Omega Station and stop this evil man?"

And still Danny was silent.

"If you don't go," I said to my robot buddy, "I'll go alone."

I meant that. And Danny knew that I did.

"You'll just get into trouble going alone," Danny said. "I guess I better go too and look after Jack."

Dr. Atkins relaxed. "Good. I knew I could count on you. Now before we make any more plans, we have to get in touch with the Jameson family."

# 5 The Road to Omega Station

There was no time to go back to our house. So Dr. Atkins got in touch with our folks over the Vue/Phone.

"What kind of mission are Jack and Danny going on?" Dad asked.

"A very important one," Dr. Atkins said.

"Will it take long?" Mom asked.

"I hope they can accomplish the mission in less than a week," Dr. Atkins said.

"You do know that Jack is in school right now," Dad said.

"I'll program Danny to work with him in all his subjects."

"Jack is *very* weak in arithmetic," Mom said.

"I'll make sure Danny is strong there."

"Just where will they be going?" asked Dad.

"Their first stop is C.O.L.A.R.," said Dr. Atkins. (He didn't know where our second stop—Omega Station—was.) "They'll be among friends on C.O.L.A.R."

"Isn't C.O.L.A.R. a few months ahead of us?" Mom asked.

What a question, I thought. I wondered what Mom was getting at.

"Yes, I believe the planet of C.O.L.A.R. is about three months ahead of us," Dr. Atkins said.

"Then I think Jack better take some hay fever pills with him. It's probably late August there now."

Hay fever pills? I tried not to laugh. What a thing to think of!

"I'll see that Jack takes hay fever pills with him, Mrs. Jameson," Dr. Atkins reassured Mom.

And then each of us got on the Vue/Phone and said good-bye and told Mom and Dad not to worry.

"I'll look after Jack," Danny said.

"And I'll look after Danny," I said.

And finally that was done.

The rest consisted of making final plans with Dr. Atkins—him checking out one of my rear teeth once more—and soon after that it was off to C.O.L.A.R.

C.O.L.A.R. is a small planet that drifted into the Earth system some years ago. The first time Danny and I went to C.O.L.A.R.—quite by accident—its surface was barren, treeless, and there were lots of holes that looked as if they'd been made by meteor-ites.

This time we skimmed over a surface as beautiful as the Earth's. There were meadows and hills, brooks and streams and ponds; we zoomed down over neat roads and small cottages, over baseball diamonds, football fields, soccer fields, tennis courts . . .

And then ahead of us we saw the towers of C.O.L.A.R. City, with its streets and buildings and swimming pools.

In the middle of the city was a spaceport. A crowd of robot boys and girls were down there waving to us. Some were holding up signs that said:

WELCOME BACK, DANNY AND JACK
ABOUT TIME
HELLO TO JACK AND DANNY FROM JOE ELEVEN
HAPPY LANDINGS TO JACK AND DANNY
WELCOME BACK TO C.O.L.A.R., JACK AND DANNY

I had to laugh. "This is sure a lot different from the first time we came here."

Danny smiled. "Just about the opposite, I think."

Dr. Atkins's pilot fired the retro-rockets and the Atkins spaceship glided into a smooth landing. Spider legs came down, and then the ramp. The pilot—

an Atkins robot—shook hands with us. He knew a little about our mission. "Good luck to you both," he said.

Outside, the crowd of robot boys and girls rushed to the ramp. Some of the faces were familiar.

"It's good to see you guys again."

"How are things on Earth?"

"Doesn't C.O.L.A.R. look different?"

"Did you hear? Someone's robotnapping our citizens."

"Does Dr. Atkins know where Ted Eight is?"

"And Sally Five?"

"And Barbara Two?"

"And Sam Ten?"

"And Bob Three? He was the last one to be missing."

Danny and I glanced at each other. They didn't know. How could they, of course? They soon would.

"Things are really scary here," a robot girl said sadly.

"Hey, Jack," one robot boy hollered at me, "can you still walk like a robot?"

That, at least, was a cheerful question I could answer right off. And I answered it by walking stiff-in-the-knee down the ramp and into the crowd.

They laughed, slapped me on the back, we shook hands, hugged . . .

And then we came face to face with our best friends on C.O.L.A.R.: Jeff One, tall, sixteen years old, the robot who had founded C.O.L.A.R.; Carl Three, who was really a walking computer, chunky, serious-faced, he knew just about everything, or could find it out in a hurry—and Ann Two, who had once saved our lives. She was brown-haired, pretty, spunky, and had a smiling face.

Now she greeted me with: "Hello, human being who walks like a robot."

"Hello, robot who looks like a human," I said to her.

We hugged. And Ann hugged Danny, stepped back and held him at arms' length, looking from one of us to the other, smiling. "You two look more like each other than before. You *are* Danny, aren't you?" she said to Danny.

"I think so," Danny said with a straight face.

I shook hands with Jeff and with Carl, and then Jeff announced to the crowd of robot kids surrounding us that "Jack and Danny need some rest now," and he ushered us through the throng of well-wishers and over to C.O.L.A.R. Control.

A year ago C.O.L.A.R. Control was a huge underground room with spiraling ramps. Now the spiraling ramps were in a large building in the heart of C.O.L.A.R. City.

On the ramps were generators, mobile battery

chargers, computers, terminals, Vue/Screens, Vue/Phones, and wires leading in almost every direction. A dozen robot boys and girls were keeping their eyes on the instruments, monitoring the energy levels of all the citizens of C.O.L.A.R.

"It looks good, Jeff," I said.

"Thanks, Jack," Jeff said, "but none of this has prevented some of our citizens from getting robot-napped. I take it you know that five of our friends are missing: Sally Five, Barbara Two, Sam Ten, Ted Eight, and Bob Three."

"We know," Danny said. "That's why we're here." And then Danny and I told them about Bob Three.

Jeff, Ann, and Carl were silent.

"The important thing," I said, "is that Bob Three gave us important information before he stopped functioning."

I described to them how Bob Three had been fishing when the strange red-and-black spaceship landed nearby, and Sally Five and Ted Eight popped out of it and talked him into going off with them.

"Wait till I get my hands on those two," Jeff said grimly.

"Maybe they couldn't help themselves, Jeff," said Danny. "Maybe they were reprogrammed at Omega Station by a man named Otto Drago."

"Omega Station," Carl said. "Hmmm . . ." He reached over and pushed some buttons on a computer. The terminal blinked three times:

NO DATA

NO DATA

NO DATA

"There's no such place in our Earth system," Carl said.

"Try Otto Drago," Jeff said.

Once more Carl punched some buttons. This time the terminal produced the following words:

OTTO DRAGO . . . SCIENTIST, ENGINEER,
ASSISTED IN DEVELOPMENT AND
DESIGN OF PROTOTYPE ATKINS ROBOTS.
FIRED FROM EMPLOYMENT BY LEOPOLD ATKINS.
DISAPPEARED TEN YEARS AGO.
WHEREABOUTS TODAY UNKNOWN.
THAT IS ALL.

"He's on Omega Station," Ann said, "wherever that is." She turned to us. "How are we going to find Omega Station and this terrible Drago person?"

"Dr. Atkins has a plan," Danny said, and then the two of us told them Dr. Atkins's plan for locating Omega Station. Which, Dr. Atkins believed, would mean locating Otto Drago.

[41]

They were silent when we finished. Ann shook her head. "That's pretty dangerous for you, Jack."

"Maybe. But if Dr. Atkins is correct, we have no choice. Drago seems to be able to reprogram an Atkins robot any way he wants. He couldn't do that to me. And he'd be thinking he had because I can imitate a robot perfectly."

"I know that," Ann said blushing, remembering how I had once fooled her.

"All that's fine," Jeff said curtly (very much like Dr. Atkins, I thought, and not surprising because Jeff had been Dr. Atkins's very own robot a while back), "but what can you do alone about capturing this Drago?"

"I won't be alone," I said. "You'll all follow me to Omega Station. I'll be in touch with you."

"How? You don't have a belly-button radio like a real Atkins robot," Jeff said.

"Dr. Atkins has fixed me up with something almost as good."

"What's that?" Carl asked.

"A radio inside my mouth."

"Let's see," Ann said.

I opened my mouth wide and said: "Ocker Akin a uck a ahser ayo a un a ack eeth," which is what "Dr. Atkins has stuck a laser radio to one of my back teeth" sounds like if you say it with your mouth wide open. Try it.

Jeff, Ann, and Carl understood what I said, but they still didn't believe me. They peered in my mouth, though, and they saw the tiny laser radio.

"I turn it on by flicking my tongue against the tooth," I said.

"Dr. Atkins is a genius," Jeff said.

"He thinks so too," I laughed.

"OK," Jeff said, "you turn the radio on by slapping the tip of your tongue against it. What do you say over it?"

"I don't know what I'll say over it because I don't know anything about Omega Station or Otto Drago. First things first, Jeff. And the first thing is for me to get robotnapped by Ted and Sally just the way Bob Three did. Dr. Atkins says I must go to the same pond at which Bob Three was fishing. And do some fishing there. He's sure they'll come back there looking for another lone robot to robotnap."

"And where are we to be?" Ann asked.

"In a spaceship in C.O.L.A.R. City ready to take off," Danny said. "You'll be watching everything on a Vue/Screen."

"What Vue/Screen? How will we see you?" Carl, ever practical, asked.

"You'll have to hang a camera on a nearby tree and hide it behind some leaves. Then you'll have a first-class view of a robotnapping. You'll also be able to hear what's going on because I'll have my tooth radio turned to SEND, and I'll repeat everything he says."

"I don't like it, Jack. It's too risky," Ann said.

"Maybe, but we have no choice, Ann," said Jeff. He turned to Danny and me. "All right, Jack is robotnapped. He's in a spaceship, the same spaceship that Bob Three was napped off in. How do we follow him?"

"Exhaust sensors," Danny said. "You follow the Omega Station spaceship's exhaust. And you follow it right to Omega Station."

"You make it sound simple," Ann said.

"It is simple," I said.

"Too simple," Ann said. "Dr. Atkins stays on Earth dreaming up a simple plan that puts your life in danger in outer space. Carl, what are the chances of this plan succeeding?"

Carl punched some more computer buttons. "Hmmm . . ." He studied numbers flashing on the terminal. "That plan has a twenty-five percent chance of succeeding," he announced.

"Dreadful," Ann said. "And what are the chances of Jack coming through it alive?"

More button pushing. More "hmmms" from Carl. And then he announced that I had a ten percent chance of coming through alive.

I must say that at that moment I wished Carl and his computer had been with us back on Earth when

Dr. Atkins proposed this whole crazy mission to Omega Station. But it was too late to back out now.

"I think Dr. Atkins's plan is terrible," Ann said. "I think we ought to think up something different."

"Like what?" Jeff challenged her.

"I don't know."

"Look," I said, "if Dr. Atkins could have thought of a safer plan, he would have. Let's give this one a try."

"We're not the ones giving it a try, Jack," Ann said, "you are. It will be your life, not ours. Isn't that right, Danny?"

"No," Danny said, "it will be the lives of all the robots if Jack fails."

"You're his robot buddy, his brother," Ann said astonished. "Do *you* think Jack ought to go on this mission?"

Danny was silent a moment. He looked at me. "Yes," he said quietly, "he has to try it. No other human could bring it off. And I have to be as close to him as I can. Because at some moment on Omega Station, I'm going to change places with Jack. Dr. Atkins is positive about that."

"That just puts two of you in danger," said Ann.

"Where we belong," I said cheerfully. "Listen, Ann, Dr. Atkins said you would lend me a fishing rod. Will you?"

"Yes," Ann said sadly.

# 6  Robotnapped!

The best thing about fishing is that once you drop your line in the water, you can forget about everything else. And that is what happened to me.

I started fishing for real from the shore of the little pond on C.O.L.A.R. The spot from where Bob Three had been lured into the Omega Station spaceship by Ted Eight and Sally Five.

*My* lure was a green wriggler that Ann had in her tackle box. My little backpack with the hay fever pills my mother insisted on my taking was leaning against a tree.

Up in that same tree Carl had hidden a camera, so that the others sitting in their spaceship could watch me fish and also watch Ted and Sally robotnap me.

Danny had been the last one to leave me by the pond.

"Jack," he warned, "don't forget. You've got to walk stiff-in-the-knee from now on."

"I won't forget. And you guys don't forget to follow us when we take off."

"We won't. And you remember about that radio. Stay in touch. It may not be possible if we're too far apart in space, but when we all get to Omega

Station, we'll be able to hear you again. And we'll be able to hear you right here when they land."

"I know. Listen, Danny, don't worry. I'm all right. I'm not scared."

"I know you're not," Danny said. "And that's what worries me most."

"Hey, cut it out. I'll see you later. I want to get some fishing in before they robotnap me."

And that's what I did while waiting for Ted and Sally to arrive in the red-and-black spaceship. I fished. Right off I got a bite. And seconds later I caught a small perch.

I tossed it back. It was too small.

I got a few more bites, and then something really big took my lure. It almost pulled me into the pond. I hoped they were watching this on their Vue/Screen. This was exciting.

I gave the fish some more line, and he took it. And then I played him, reeling in, letting him fight, tire himself, reel in some more. He broke water with a high leap. It was a big brown trout. Jeff had stocked C.O.L.A.R.'s ponds a year ago with baby trout.

This one was a beauty and a real fighter. I must have been fifteen minutes working him toward shore, and when I got him within a few feet of me, I could see he was at least twenty-four inches long. And it suddenly dawned on me that I had no landing net.

[ 48 ]

How was I going to scoop him up? I couldn't lift him up by the line. He was too heavy. He'd break the rod.

I couldn't grab him with one hand and hold the rod with the other. He was too slippery for that. I really needed four hands. What could I do?

"Can I help you?" a voice behind me said.

I started to say "You bet you can" when I turned and saw just who it was talking to me.

It was a little fat man with pop eyes and big ears. He had a friendly smile on a comical face. It was a face I had seen on Dr. Atkins's Vue/Screen just yesterday.

It belonged to Dr. Otto Drago!

Oh, no, I thought, this isn't how it's supposed to be. A red-and-black spaceship is supposed to land nearby. Ted Eight and Sally Five are supposed to jump out and talk me into going to Omega Station with them.

Where did he come from? Where's the ship? Dr. Atkins's plan is already starting to go wrong.

Otto Drago beamed at me. He looked very friendly.

"You seem to be having troubles bringing in your trout, my young robot friend. Can I give you a hand?" He giggled. "Perhaps even two hands?"

Chills went down my spine.

"Uh . . . yeah . . . sure, I mean thanks."

Otto Drago waddled around me and went into the shallow water with his pants and all and grabbed my trout with two strong pudgy hands. He brought it to me.

"A true beauty," he exclaimed.

I removed the lure from the fish's mouth.

"You must have a bag for your fish," he said.

"Yes," I said, without thinking, "right there against the tree."

That was dumb. My hay fever pills were in the bag. Robots didn't need pills. He'd see them and get suspicious.

I closed my eyes, waiting for him to discover my pills. But nothing happened. I opened my eyes.

He had just put the fish inside my pack without looking. Now he stood up and waddled past me to the water's edge and washed his hands in the water.

I watched him, thinking: where was the spaceship? What had happened to Ted and Sally? Were Danny, Jeff, Ann, and Carl watching this now? But they weren't hearing anything.

Turn on your radio, dummy!

I flicked the tip of my tongue against the back tooth and felt the tiny laser radio click on.

"You know, my young friend," Otto Drago said, beaming at me, "I don't think I've ever seen an Atkins robot catch a fish as well as you."

Was he suspicious? Testing me to see if I really was an Atkins robot?

I marched up to him stiff-in-the-knee and boasted: "Oh, Dr. Atkins programmed me to be a great fisherman. He said we robots would need fresh fish for any human visitors to C.O.L.A.R."

I could tell he was reassured. He smiled. "Dr. Atkins thinks of everything, doesn't he?" He looked around carefully. "Do you always fish alone?"

"Yes, sir. It's hard to catch fish when others are around. Especially robots who aren't programmed to fish. But you, sir, you are not a robot, are you?"

Otto Drago chuckled. "Unfortunately not. There's no machine I admire more than an Atkins robot. Nor any human being I admire more than the man who invented them—Leopold Atkins. Let me introduce myself. I am . . ." he produced a card from his pocket and handed it to me.

I read:

DR. OTTO DRAGO
· DIRECTOR ·
OMEGA STATION
"A DELIGHTFUL SUMMER CAMP FOR ATKINS ROBOTS"

"You run a summer camp, Dr. Drago?" I asked loudly, wanting to make sure Danny and the others caught the name.

"Indeed, I do," said Otto Drago, taking the card back from me, "and several Atkins robots are there already enjoying the lovely facilities. Absolutely free of charge. And now that you know *my* name, may I ask you yours?"

"My name is Danny One, sir."

"Danny One," Otto Drago repeated, "a fine name. Excellent. Well, Danny One, you're a very lucky robot. Since you're the first Atkins robot I've met on C.O.L.A.R. today, let me give *you* my absolutely free offer. No strings attached. No proof of purchase necessary. And that offer, sir, is: a trip to the delights, beauties, and heavenly pleasures of Omega Station, a place where no work is ever done, chores are unheard of, a place where the guiding principle of life is pleasure and where robots never, never, never need those irritating and time-consuming battery charges. Does all this intrigue you, sir? For if it does, then Omega Station is the place for you."

"Wow," I said. "A place where there are no battery charges. Omega Station sounds great."

"It *is* great," Otto Drago said, leaning toward me, like a super salesman. He smelled a little of onions, I thought, but I had to be careful not to let him know that, since robots aren't supposed to be able to smell things.

"And if you doubt me, Danny One, come with me and see the beauties of Omega Station for yourself."

"Just where is Omega Station anyway?" I asked loudly.

His answer could be important.

Otto Drago's eyes twinkled as he recited:

> *Behind the Moon*
> *Around a star*
> *Not very close*
> *Not very far*

Great, I thought, a poet. A real help.

"How did you get here, Dr. Drago? I didn't even hear you arrive."

Otto Drago waved a hand nonchalantly toward the little hill behind the tree that had the camera hidden in it. "I have a conveyance parked nearby, Danny One."

And that was when I made my first mistake. I had been doing beautifully till then.

"What's a conveyance?" I asked.

Those jovial little eyes of Otto Drago immediately narrowed suspiciously. I realized right away I'd said something wrong.

"Every Atkins robot," he said softly, "is bright enough to know what a conveyance is."

Danny, help me, I prayed.

"Oh," I stalled, "a conveyance. I thought you said a con*day*ance. I thought it was some kind of dance.

We robots who have to walk stiff-in-the-knee don't know much about dancing. But conveyance . . . that's different. Why, everyone knows what a conveyance is. (Everyone but me!) Why, a conveyance is nothing but . . ."

A little tone went off inside my mouth and I heard Danny's voice whispering in my head: ". . . a ride, a car, a spaceship. Whatever gets you from one place to another . . ."

". . . a ride, a car, a spaceship. Whatever gets you from one place to another," I repeated.

The suspicious look vanished from Otto Drago's face. Once again he was all phony smiles. "Exactly," he said. "And I've parked my conveyance just the other side of the hill. Come along, Danny One."

"Just the other side of the hill" meant it was out of range of the camera Carl had hung on the tree nearby. I'd better tell them where we were headed.

"So your conveyance is just the other side of the hill," I repeated loudly.

"I just said that," Otto Drago snapped. And then he remembered he was supposed to act kind and friendly. He smiled and said: "Better take your pack with you. *You* won't need any fish for dinner, being a robot, but . . ." He smacked his lips, "*I* could use a nice trout dinner tonight. You won't mind giving me your trout, will you, Danny One?"

"Oh, no, not at all," I said, thinking that what I'd really like to give him was a hit over the head with the fish.

I picked up my green backpack with the hay fever pills and the fish and my micro food and went off with Otto Drago, remembering to walk stiff-in-the-knee.

Otto Drago watched me approvingly. "You know, Danny One, one of the terrible problems of being human is that we have to eat all the time . . ."

Judging from his tummy, he ate more than all the time, I thought.

". . . that's one reason robots are better off than humans."

"I guess you're right, sir," I said, and thought: it's time to tell Danny where we are now. The camera couldn't see us here.

I said loudly: "I really like climbing over little hills."

Otto Drago looked amused. "Do you? You're an unusual robot then, Danny One. Most robots don't like to climb at all."

I knew why. It's hard walking stiff-in-the-knee.

"Oh," I said loudly, "a small hill near a pond like this is no problem at all. It's always fun when you get to the top," I puffed, "and see . . ."

I stopped. We were at the top. There in a clearing

on the other side of the hill was a small red-and-black spaceship. The exact spaceship Bob Three had described.

". . . a red-and-black spaceship," I finished my sentence.

"Isn't it a beauty?" Otto Drago said, his eyes gleaming. "I bought it used in Kappa Galaxy some years ago. It flies beautifully. You can also fly it silently; it has sound absorbers. Come along, Danny One. We've no time to waste."

Sound absorbers? That was why I hadn't heard it approach.

I stumbled down the hill. It was harder walking stiff-in-the-knee downhill than uphill. But somehow I managed.

The radio tone sounded in my mouth. And I heard Danny's voice in my head. "Ask him if he flies it alone. Jeff wants to know what has happened to Ted and Sally."

"Do you fly it all by yourself?" I puffed.

"Indeed I do. I also have pilots, but right now they're a little . . . shall we say . . . run down? I've given them a few days off. They're lying by the beautiful swimming pool on Omega Station resting up. Up the ramp we go, Danny One."

Otto Drago was doing everything but pushing me up.

"It's a small ship," I said loudly, "and I see four retro-rockets. Is it fast?"

Carl would need this information for their ship's computer.

Otto Drago looked at me curiously. "Danny One, you ask odd questions."

"I'm a spaceship buff," I said quickly.

"Well," he said, "when pushed it can do a hundred thousand miles per hour."

"Wow," I said loudly, "a hundred thousand miles per hour. What kind of fuel does it use?"

This was important, for the answer would enable

Carl to set the exhaust sensor on the C.O.L.A.R. spaceship.

"Vaporized carbon, and that, my young robot friend, ends question-and-answer time."

With a polite but firm hand Otto Drago ushered me inside the Omega Station spaceship, closed and locked the outer and inner doors.

"Vaporized carbon," I said loudly.

"Got it. Thanks," Danny whispered inside my head.

Otto Drago looked at me curiously. "Are you hard of hearing, Danny One?"

"No, sir," I said, and sat down next to the pilot's seat.

He frowned. "You repeat everything I say. Don't you hear me the first time?"

"I guess it's just a habit, Dr. Drago."

For a split second the veil of good humor dropped from the little fat man's face. His eyes were hard and cruel. "A habit I'll cure you of at Omega Station," he said softly. And then he laughed, and the phony mask of friendliness dropped down over his face again. "Habits can be programmed and reprogrammed." He pushed a button and the ship's engines roared into life.

I clicked off my tooth radio. There could be no more radio contact now. I just had to hope that the others would be able to follow us.

Otto Drago smiled at me. "Don't look so worried, Danny One. I assure you . . . you will love Omega Station."

"I'm sure I will," I lied.

I had a sinking feeling in my stomach as the ship rose from the surface of C.O.L.A.R. and we shot off into outer space.

# 7 Obstacle Course in Space

Later Danny told me what was going on in their spaceship while Otto Drago was pushing me into his.

Ann and Jeff were having an argument.

Ann was for stopping the whole mission right then and there. "Nothing's going right," she said. "We expected Ted and Sally and now there's Otto Drago himself. I say we fly to the pond and arrest him right away."

"On what charges?" Jeff asked. "And if we do that, how are we ever going to find Ted Eight and Sally Five, Sam Ten and Barbara Two? We don't even know where Omega Station is."

"It's too risky for Jack right now," Ann said.

"Sure it's risky," Jeff agreed. "But he's only one person. Not even a robot at that. Our whole planet's existence may be at stake."

"Jeff, how can you even think like that? Jack came all the way from Earth to help us."

"Then give him a chance to help us!" Jeff turned to Carl. "What do you think?"

Carl blinked through his thick glasses. "I'm just an information source. Ask Danny."

"We'll let Danny decide."

"No, we won't," said Jeff. "He's Jack's buddy and brother."

"Carl won't vote," Ann said. "I vote against the mission; you vote for it. Danny is the only one who can decide."

Jeff hesitated. Then he shrugged. "All right. We'll let you decide, Danny. Risking Jack's life or letting this Otto Drago pick off our friends one by one. Which is it to be?"

Danny was silent. He told me later it was a hard moment for him. But what made him decide ultimately was his ability to put himself inside my skin. Knowing what I'd like. How I'd vote.

"I vote for going on with the mission," he said at last. "But when we get to Omega Station, Jack and I change places right away."

"After the reprogramming of Jack fails," Jeff said.

"Agreed."

"They're off the ground now!" Carl was scanning a Vue/Screen reading of the skies over C.O.L.A.R.

A tiny blip was rising from the bottom of the green screen.

They all watched the little white blip slowly rise.

"We'll have to wait till they're off the screen," said Carl. "Otherwise they can see us following them on their scanner."

It felt like forever, Danny told me later, waiting for the Omega Station spaceship's blip to leave the screen.

"It looks like they're heading for the Moon," Carl said.

"Drago could be trying to throw anyone following off the track," Jeff said.

The little white blip was at the top edge of the screen.

Jeff started up the C.O.L.A.R. ship's motors.

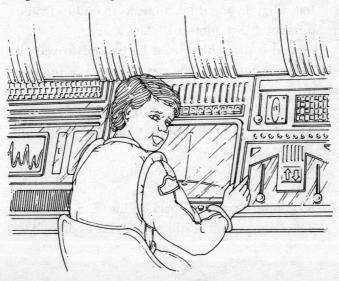

"They're off the screen!" Carl said.

"Turn up the sensor, Carl. We're off too."

The C.O.L.A.R. spaceship lifted off.

Now they would be flying a route charted by the information the exhaust sensor was feeding into the flight computer.

The exhaust sensor was really a little pipe that stuck out from the belly of the ship and sniffed out gasses and heat molecules like a hungry dog.

The computer got a readout from the exhaust sensor right away.

"They *are* heading for the Moon," Ann said.

The reading from the Omega Station spaceship was strong and clear. Below them, C.O.L.A.R. faded to a small dot. They began to relax. At least they were on the right trail.

"Jeff, what do you think it means that Otto Drago robotnapped Jack himself?" Ann asked.

Jeff said it probably meant he had destroyed all the other robots and now was finding new ones to destroy.

"But why?" Ann asked. "Why does he do this?"

"That's one of the things we've got to find·out for Dr. Atkins," Danny said.

"What else did Dr. Atkins tell you to do?" Ann asked.

"Stop him. Bring him back to Earth, if we can."

"The Omega ship is still on a direct approach to

the Moon," Carl sang out from the computer console. "It is approaching the main industrial highway."

"What I don't understand," said Ann, "is if this horrible person wants to destroy Atkins robots, why doesn't he just attack C.O.L.A.R. instead of picking us off one by one."

"Dr. Atkins thinks that maybe he doesn't want to destroy robots, but he's using them for something that in the end does destroy them," Danny said.

"What is he using them for?" Ann asked.

"That we don't know, but it's got to be bad."

"The Omega ship is now crossing the industrial highway," Carl sang out.

"That's where Bob Three was found," Danny said quietly.

Everyone was silent. Just the purring sounds of the instruments aboard the ship. Outside, the silent rush of dark outer space.

In a few moments, though, they began to see traffic out the control windows. Air trucks on the regular Earth–Moon run. A shuttle carrying miners back to Earth from a week's work on the Moon.

There were shuttles from the space colonies. One from J Colony, a big 'J' painted on its side, flew alongside them for a while before turning toward another colony.

(I've put a map of the Earth system on page 66

# THE EARTH SYSTEM

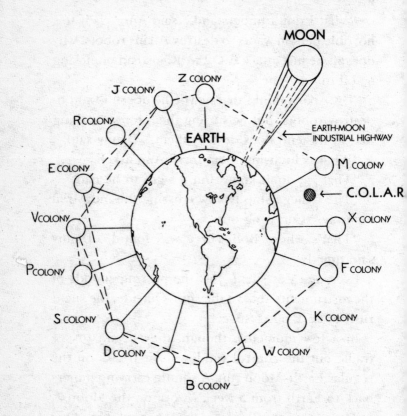

MOON

Z COLONY

J COLONY

R COLONY

EARTH

E COLONY

EARTH-MOON
INDUSTRIAL HIGHWAY

V COLONY

M COLONY

C.O.L.A.R

X COLONY

P COLONY

F COLONY

S COLONY

K COLONY

D COLONY

W COLONY

B COLONY

– – – – – SHUTTLE ROUTES BETWEEN SPACE COLONIES

———— ROUTES BETWEEN SPACE COLONIES AND EARTH

where you can see the Earth, the Moon, the fourteen space colonies, and some of the connecting routes between them.)

Danny pointed to a light blinking off the port bow. "What's that?" he asked.

Jeff looked up from the controls. "Oh, that's just a warning blinker. There are all sorts of obstructions in space. Those lights are there to warn spaceships to go around the obstructions. Most of the obstructions are old air-pumping stations. The humans who first set up the space colonies lived on those platforms enclosed in a plastic shield into which air was pumped."

And today they were just orbiting junkyards, Danny thought.

They shot by the obstruction. It was immense.

During the time they were tracking the Omega spaceship, they saw three more warning blinkers.

"Drago's got to be past the normal Moon approach now," Jeff said, staring at the flight computer.

"He's making a starboard turn, Jeff," Carl said, studying the sensor readout. "I think he's going around the Moon. We'll be turning too, Jeff, in seventy-three seconds."

"When will we get back in radio contact with Jack?" Ann asked.

"We've got to be within ten miles of Jack for that," Jeff said.

Something very large passed over their heads. They looked up. It was the Super Inter-galaxy Transport, filled with people. Some waved down at them. Ann waved back.

Another obsolete pumping station loomed off the port bow. They gave its blinking light signal a wide berth.

Now they were swinging back toward the Moon but on a course that would soon take them to the dark side.

Danny peered at the moonscape below. There were huge plastic domes on this, the lighted side of the Moon. The domes shielded factory workers engaged in a variety of industrial operations. All kinds of metals were mined, processed, and smelted down on the Moon.

As they skimmed the domes, Danny could see within them trucks, cranes, all kinds of industrial equipment. Some of the domes were twenty miles across.

In seconds, though, they were past the area of the domes and were now flying into shadow, into the dark side of the Moon.

Carl's voice sounded nervous. "Jeff, the vapor carbon reading is getting faint. They're cutting their engines."

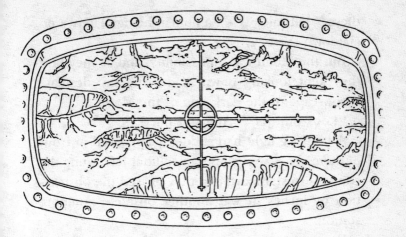

If that was true, that would be the end of everything, Danny thought. They could only follow the Omega ship by its engine exhaust.

"Stay with it, Carl," Jeff said. "It could be our equipment."

"No, it's not us. Our sensor's working. I tell you, Jeff, somewhere ahead of us they've cut their engines."

There was now no point in Carl reading the computer anymore. He joined them at the flight controls. They all peered into the darkness.

"They've got to be somewhere ahead of us," Jeff said.

"Could they have landed on the Moon?" Ann asked.

"Not unless Drago's built a plastic shield down

there," Jeff said. "He's a human being. There's no air down there."

But the Moon was a possibility, and as they flew they kept looking down at the rugged, desolate moonscape of the dark side of the Moon.

"Look out, Jeff!" Ann screamed.

A blinking light had suddenly appeared in front of them. They were about to collide! Jeff swung the controls to starboard and they missed the obstruction by inches. It was another obsolete pumping station.

For a moment no one said anything. "My fault," Jeff said apologetically. "I was looking at the Moon surface."

"Maybe Drago did put a dome down there," Ann said. "We ought to scout the surface. And we don't have much time."

"All right," Jeff said. He shoved in the vertical control, and the spaceship shot down toward the Moon surface. For the next few minutes they skimmed over the peaks and craters and valleys and the cracked surfaces of the Moon. They flew between mountains, with each of them peering down onto the dark surface looking for a place of habitation, a place that might be called Omega Station.

But there was nothing.

They crisscrossed the dark side of the Moon from one end to the other. Nothing. The Omega Station spaceship had fooled them. It had disappeared.

"They've got to be somewhere," Jeff said angrily. "They couldn't have vanished into thin air."

Those words of Jeff's hung like soundless weights in the cabin. Something was wrong. Danny's computer pack began clicking, silicon chips were whispering, chattering, telling him something . . . but what? What?

"Thin air," they whispered. "Thin air," they repeated. "Thin air," they screamed at him.

And then suddenly he understood.

"That last obsolete air-pumping station we almost hit," Danny yelled. "It didn't belong on the dark side of the Moon. There never were space colonies on this side of the Moon."

The others stared at him.

And Ann, who was programmed for goose pimples, got them.

Carl closed his eyes and said, "All air-pumping stations are on the bright side of the Moon. Any air-pumping station on this side was not here originally."

"Jeff!" Ann yelled. "That last blinking light! The one we almost crashed into."

But Jeff had already turned the ship about. And now they flew full speed toward that last air-pumping station—the final obstruction in space.

# 8   Omega Station

In our spaceship—the Omega Station spaceship—
everything was dark. Otto Drago had cut the engines and the cabin lights. Now we were floating
toward a light blinking in the darkness outside.

Drago wasn't paying any attention to me. He was
humming an old folk song—it sounded familiar—
and punching the radio button on his flight console
as he hummed.

Finally he stopped humming and stopped punching the button. He turned in his seat and beamed at
me.

"Well, Danny One, we are almost there."

"What is that blinking light ahead of us?" I asked.

"That, my curious little robot, is Omega Station."

It didn't look like anything but a blinking light. I

stared through the window at the darkness around it, trying to see a shape. I felt that something was happening out there, but I couldn't tell what. But as we got closer, I realized that the light was perched on top of something huge, massive, deep. It was so big it *was* the darkness. There was nothing else but it.

A huge structure in space. I began to see outlines. Wide at the top, a huge dome, and then tapering down to a narrow tip at the bottom.

A huge top orbiting in space.

And now something was moving on the dome. It was the dome itself moving . . . it was sliding back. I could hear a whirring noise.

The Omega ship inched closer and closer. Otto Drago was steering it carefully, but a little smile played on his lips.

I looked back at the dome. And then I realized what had happened. The dome had slid up and left a small opening for us to enter. Otto Drago was guiding the ship into that opening.

Inside we went.

It was a fancier version of Dad opening the garage door back home to drive his solar car in.

It was dark inside. Otto Drago brought the ship to a halt. I felt the spider legs go down, and the ramp extend outward.

Then Drago began pushing the button again.

And the dome began to slide back. I could hear the whirring noise again.

Sitting there in the dark, getting locked in like that, I began to get worried for the first time. How would the others get in? That looked to be a very special button he had been punching.

Otto Drago turned to me. "In a moment, my dear Danny One, you will see a simply splendid sight."

We were still in darkness. Darkness inside the ship, darkness outside the ship.

"Does Omega Station have lights?" I asked nervously. "I never heard of a summer camp that didn't have lights."

Otto Drago chuckled. "Oh, soon enough you'll see the light, my young robot friend. And you'll see other wonderful things too. Including a beautiful swimming pool. You'll go swimming every day here."

That was the second time he mentioned a swimming pool. Why? Robots don't usually swim. They don't enjoy swimming. Not the way humans do. Danny had told me that.

And then I remembered Bob Three's words: ". . . down . . . down . . . down . . . it was blue . . . wet . . . there was pain . . ."

Could that have been a reference to Omega Station's swimming pool? And why pain?

"Be patient, Danny One," Drago said, smiling at

me. "As soon as the dome is back in place, a connection is made, and the lights will go on. But we must stay inside the ship until the dome is secure. You see, the dome is necessary for air-breathing mortals like myself, though not necessary for splendid Atkins robots like you."

It dawned on me that, funny as it seemed, my personal safety lay in sticking close to this terrible man. Although he didn't know it, I was an air-breathing mortal too.

The whirring noise stopped. I heard a click.

And then as the great dome clicked shut, Omega Station lighted up!

I gasped. It was a fantastic sight. The spaceship was resting inside a vast roofed hall—bigger than any of the domed stadiums back home. (There were no seats, of course.) There were small houses, trees, and sidewalks, a sort of town square, and in the middle there was a large swimming pool. Along the walks there were posts on which air helmets were hanging, the kinds of air helmets we have in all the space colonies for emergency protection in case a meteorite should shatter the plastic shield. This told me that Omega Station had once been occupied by lots of people. I wondered what had happened to them.

The dome was very high. You couldn't hit a baseball to the ceiling, even if you were a major-leaguer.

Also the dome was painted black. Black, I guessed, so no one could see in and no light could leak out.

Otto Drago was looking at me amused as I looked everywhere at once.

He chuckled. "I was considering painting stars on the ceiling for robot boys and girls who like to watch stars, but I haven't had the time to do that yet. Well, what do you think of Omega Station, Danny One?"

"It's unbelievable," I said truthfully.

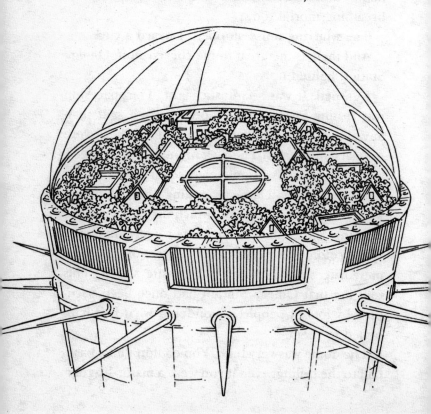

"On the contrary," he said, his eyes gleaming, "it is very believable and real and important. And it's all mine. From here I will . . ."

He stopped himself. "What am I saying? It's time to leave the ship and enroll you in our camp. You're a most unusual robot, Danny One. You have the human ability to make me talk too much."

"But, Dr. Drago," I said politely, "do I have to enroll? I mean, I'm not sure I want to enroll. I thought I was just coming here for a look around and to talk to the other C.O.L.A.R. robots who are here."

"Of course," he said smoothly. "But before you can talk to them you must undergo orientation."

I knew what orientation really meant—*reprogramming!*

"Why do I have to be oriented if I'm not staying?" I asked.

"All visitors must learn the rules of Omega Station, even," he assured me, "if they don't intend to stay."

It would be dangerous for me to object anymore.

Otto Drago opened the inner and outer door. I picked up my backpack with the pills and the fish, and followed him out onto the ramp. Luckily for me he was a couple of steps ahead of me. I say "luckily" because I forgot to walk stiff-in-the-knee. Who could remember a thing like this at a time like this?

"All this," Otto Drago said, waving his hand at the houses, the trees, the sidewalks, lights, posts, "all this is only because human beings are inefficient and cannot live in outer space without help. I'd give my eyeteeth to be a robot and not have to eat, sleep, and breathe. But, alas . . . I'm a human being."

Not much of one, I thought. But the words *eyeteeth* reminded me of something.

I poked my tongue back to the tiny laser radio and flicked it on. My only hope for escaping from here was to somehow get the others in. I sure hoped they'd been able to follow us, and that now they were close enough again for radio contact. Somehow I was going to have to tell them how Otto Drago had made the dome slide back. But how had he?

Start asking questions, I thought. And start with pointless ones.

"Why did you paint the dome black, Dr. Drago?"

"Because, Danny One, we don't want people to know about Omega Station."

"Why not?"

"Clearly if everyone knew what a delightful place this was, we would be overrun with visitors."

I took a deep breath. "I think visitors would have a hard time getting in. By the way, how *did* you get that dome to slide back?"

Otto Drago chuckled. "You ask too many questions, Danny One. Come along to the Orientation Room."

I didn't move. He'd have to be patient with me. I wasn't reprogrammed yet.

"Oh, I was programmed by Dr. Atkins to ask questions."

"Programmed to fish and ask questions," Otto Drago said, amused. "What a queer combination of things and both very inefficient uses of robotics. We'll certainly change that."

"It's OK with me," I said cheerfully, "if you tell me how you got the dome to slide back. That's all I want to know."

"A modest request. Well, my young robot friend, it's a code of notes that I radio to an activator on the dome. Now come along."

"A code of notes that you radio to an activator on the dome," I repeated loudly. "Wow." I hoped to God the others were listening. I also hoped they understood what that meant because I sure didn't.

"Your question is now answered. Come along to the Orientation Room."

"Yes, sir." I remembered just in time to walk stiff-in-the-knee down the ramp and toward a cottage that looked to be a little bigger and nicer than the others.

We passed more poles with emergency air helmets hanging from them.

I was aware of the big swimming pool in the center. It seemed to be the most important thing in Omega Station.

Over the door of the Orientation Room was a sign.

OMEGA STATION
OFFICE of ORIENTATION

O. DRAGO, DIRECTOR

"We'll have a bit of orientation first," Otto Drago said, and then he rubbed his hands together in anticipation, "and after that I'll put your trout on the fire."

"Fire?" I repeated.

"Yes, fire," Otto Drago said, beaming.

# 9  Debate in Space

Unfortunately for me, as the Omega spaceship had entered Omega Station, the C.O.L.A.R. spaceship with my friends aboard was still far away.

It was hustling back, though, darting through Moon valleys and shooting like a pea between Moon peaks, taking the quickest route back to the warning blinker.

Jeff looked at the comp-map and declared they were at the right coordinates. He pulled out the vertical control and the ship zoomed up away from the Moon surface.

"It should be fifteen seconds ahead of us," Jeff said.

"I should have thought of it at the time," Danny said. "Every second is important. God knows what could be happening to Jack inside Omega Station."

"We should all have thought of it," Ann said.

They were each peering into the darkness now, trying to spot the blinker light into which they had almost crashed earlier. They knew that if they didn't spot it in the next few seconds, they might not ever see it. They could be searching in outer space forever, one blip searching another, while the stars looked down amused at the futility of such a search.

"It's got to be around here," Jeff said.

"Are you sure about those coordinates?" Carl asked.

"I see it!" Ann yelled.

And sure enough, there it was, far off the port bow, a tiny light blinking in the darkness.

"Good for you, Ann," Jeff said, steering their craft toward it.

"Careful now, Jeff," warned Carl, "if it is one of the original air-pumping stations, it's got to be a big structure."

Jeff slowed the ship down to half-speed.

"We'll have to risk a light," he said. He flicked on a laser light beam that cut like a knife through the blackness and illuminated the outlines of an awesome structure, spinning slowly in space.

"History, Carl," Jeff ordered.

Carl's memory chips began to click. He closed his eyes and recited:

"Both human and robot engineers were employed to build the thirteen space colonies. They needed a place for the engineers to live. Large work stations were hauled into a Moon orbit. Alpha Station, Delta Station, and Gamma Station. Plastic domes were built over the top of each station to prevent meteorite damage and maintain an atmosphere for air-breathing humans.

"Inside the stations," Carl continued, "cottages were erected, also recreational facilities. Each station had a swimming pool. Below the swimming pools were the generators to pump air.

"When the thirteen space colonies were completed, the work stations were left in place. They were too expensive to dismantle. A blinking warning light was put on each to alert passing ships to this obstruction in space. That is all. The end."

Carl opened his eyes and added quietly, "I do believe they are supposed to be uninhabited, Jeff."

"Well, this one isn't," Jeff said. "Thanks, Carl."

"Carl, you didn't mention an Omega Station," Ann said.

"There is no Omega Station, Ann Two," Carl replied.

"Drago changed the name," Jeff said. "He probably towed one of the stations from the bright side of the Moon over to this side and called it Omega

Station. Why, I don't know. And I don't know how we get inside it. Anyone have any ideas on the matter?"

The C.O.L.A.R. spaceship was moving slowly along the outer surface of the dome. It presented a smooth, dark, seamless surface. There were no entrances, no openings . . .

"There has to be a way in," said Danny. "Their spaceship got in. Ours can too." He paused. "We lost track of his carbon exhaust. That meant he either stopped or cut his engines almost out."

"I'll cut ours to one-tenth speed," said Jeff.

And now they moved even more slowly, circling the dome like a dog sniffing out a bush. Its quarry was inside. How to get at it.

And finally they completed a full turn around it.

"We've got to do something quickly," Ann said.

"Carl," Jeff said, "what do you think?"

"We could blast our way in using the laser cannon," Carl said.

"I was thinking that too," Jeff said, with a glance at Danny.

"That would be the end of Dr. Drago right away," Carl said. "The air inside would leak out and he would die immediately."

"And so would Jack," Danny said, looking directly at Jeff.

[85]

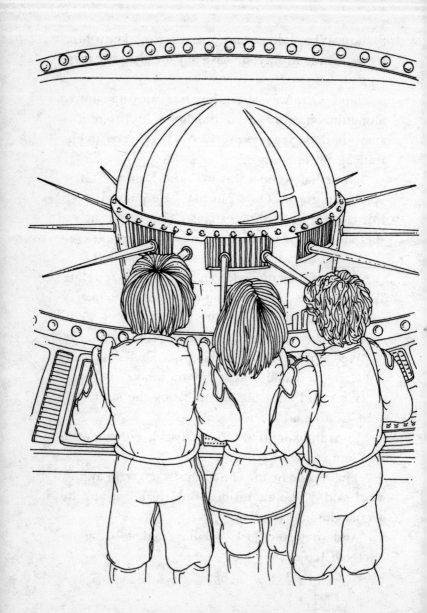

"We can't have that," Ann said.

"All right," Jeff said, "then you two come up with a better idea."

"For starters," Ann said, "I suggest we don't panic."

"Who's panicking?" Jeff said, irritated. "The fact is we've got to destroy Dr. Otto Drago before he destroys C.O.L.A.R."

"But we're not going to destroy Jack in order to kill Drago," Ann replied.

"Then suggest something else," Jeff said.

But Ann couldn't.

Danny said: "Let's turn on our radios. Jack could be trying to get in touch with us."

"Good idea," said Ann.

It wasn't a good idea, it was a desperate idea, as Danny said later.

They turned on their belly-button radios, but nothing came out of them.

"Unless someone comes up with a good idea very soon," Jeff said softly, "I'm going to make the decision to blast our way in."

Danny stared at the big dome ahead of them. Somehow the Omega Station spaceship had got inside it. There had to be a way.

"Jeff," he said, "don't rush. We can figure this out."

"I'm not rushing, Danny," Jeff said quietly. "If I

were really rushing I would have blasted a hole in there already. But you mustn't forget: at this moment the lives of Ted Eight, Sally Five, Sam Ten, and Barbara Two may be at stake. I am responsible for them. I know this is hard on you, Danny. Jack is your buddy. He has been a buddy to us all. But any way you look at it, Danny, it is still the life of one person versus the lives of four robots—not to mention the very future of C.O.L.A.R. if we don't destroy this man."

"We're not going to blast a hole in that dome," Ann said determinedly.

"You're not being reasonable, Ann Two," Jeff said. He looked baffled. "All Atkins robots are programmed to be reasonable."

"I am being reasonable," Ann said. "It just seems to me that if we have to kill someone as good as Jack Jameson to save C.O.L.A.R., then C.O.L.A.R. may not be worth saving."

"That's your opinion."

"Secondly, being reasonable is understanding that where one spaceship has gone, another can go too."

"Then tell us where to go."

Ann was silent. "I can't," she admitted.

"Exactly," said Jeff. "You can't. I can't. Carl can't. Danny can't. So I'm going to make a decision. Unless someone comes up with a way for us to get inside **Omega Station** without blasting our way in, then in exactly ten seconds I'm going to release a laser shell."

And then to underline the seriousness of his intentions, Jeff turned the laser cannon switch to ON.

"You can't do this, Jeff," Ann protested, "we don't even know for sure that this *is* Omega Station."

"So much the better for Jack if it isn't. Ten . . ." Jeff was starting his countdown.

"Carl," Ann said, "we can't let him do this."

"Nine," said Jeff, and sighted the laser cannon.

"I agree with Jeff, Ann," Carl said quietly. "The life of one person is not worth the lives of four robots!"

"Eight," said Jeff.

"Jeff," Danny said, "let me go out there and investigate that dome close up."

"There's no time for that," Jeff said. "Seven."

Ann threw herself at Jeff, trying to knock him away from the cannon trigger. Jeff caught her wrist and stopped her.

"No, Ann," he said gently but firmly, "we've lost Bob Three. We're probably losing Sam Ten and Barbara Two, Ted Eight and Sally Five right now. We're not taking any more chances with Dr. Otto Drago. Six."

Ann started to cry.

"Five," said Jeff.

Danny twisted his belly-button radio to SEND. "Jack," he called out. "Jack Jameson. Can you hear me? Jack Jameson, can you hear me?"

There was no answer.

"Four," said Jeff.

"Everyone must go to the back of the ship," Carl said. "There will be a shockwave from the explosion."

"Jack," Danny cried out, "come in if you can hear me."

"Three," Jeff said.

Carl took Ann to the back of the ship.

"Jack!" Danny yelled.

"Two."

"Jack!!"

"One and . . ."

"Fire?" said a voice.

But it wasn't Jeff's voice. It was mine.

## 10 Brother Shock

"Yes, fire!" Otto Drago said. "As soon as I finish your orientation, Danny One, I shall cook your trout over a fire and then eat it. Now give me your backpack, and I'll put the fish in a cooler for now."

There was no way I was going to give him my pack and take a chance on his finding my hay fever pills. So I took the trout out myself and handed it to him.

The little fat man's mouth watered at the sight. "I'll be right back. You sit in that chair and make yourself comfortable."

We were in the Orientation Room—a small room in the Director's cottage. There was a large chair that looked like a dentist's chair back home: white, steel, with a lot of wires attached to it. Alongside the big chair was a computer.

I sat down on the chair. Otto Drago beamed at me from the doorway, the fish in his hands. "Comfy?" he asked.

"Just fine," I reassured him.

"Good. I'll return in a moment."

I counted to three silently after he left, and then I whispered: "Danny, are you there?"

For I'd heard a confusion of voices inside my head but hadn't dared to talk into my tooth radio till Otto Drago left the room.

"Yes, Jack. We're here. Right outside the dome," Danny said. "How do we get inside?"

"The dome is hinged. It slides back."

"Ask him how you get it to slide back." I heard Jeff's voice in the background.

"Tell Jeff that Drago pushed a radio button. It's a code of notes, he told me, that works an activator on the dome."

"A code of notes?" Danny asked. "What does that mean?"

"I don't know."

"You've got to find out, Jack," Ann Two said. "Where are you now?"

"In his office. He's going to reprogram me. He calls it orientation, but it's really . . ."

I stopped. The door had opened, and Otto Drago stood there frowning at me.

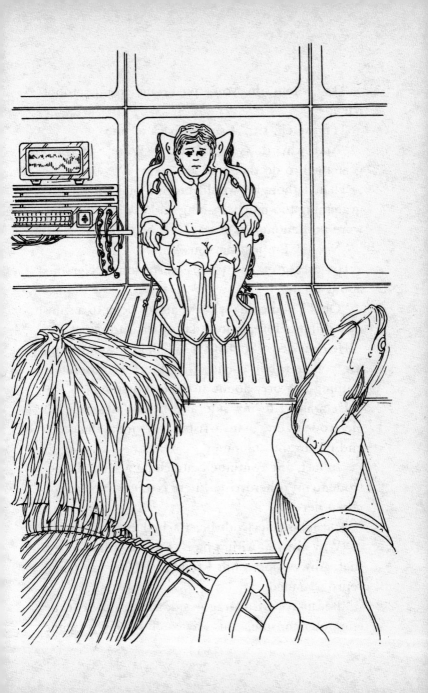

"To whom do you speak, my young robot friend?"

"To myself, sir," I smiled back at him.

"And why do you do that? Were you programmed to do that too?"

That, I thought, would be one odd bit of programming too much. Fishing and asking questions were odd enough as it was.

"No, sir. I'm just nervous."

His eyes grew even more suspicious. "Nervous about what?"

"Oh," I said casually, "I've never been to a summer camp before. I don't know what to expect."

He chuckled. "So that's it? Well, I can assure you, my young robot friend, that there is absolutely nothing to worry about at Omega Station."

He walked to my side and began attaching an electrode to one of my wrists. The wire at the other end ran to the computer.

"In fact," he continued, attaching a second electrode to my other wrist, "there is much to be happy about here."

And a third electrode he attached to my forehead.

"Why are you wiring me?" I asked. I had to ask that. Any Atkins robot would know he was being reprogrammed.

"Because," Otto Drago said, sitting down at the computer console, "this way you'll remember some

[ 94 ]

of the rules of Omega Station. Every place—even paradise—has its rules."

He began pushing buttons. Lights went on all over the console.

"But I think already that it's a great place, Dr. Drago. And you know what I like best about it?"

"What's that?" He had finished at the console and now had swiveled in his chair and sat facing me, ready to begin the process of reprogramming.

"No one can get in unless they have that code of notes you mentioned."

"Exactly right," he said. "Now I am going to tell you all about Omega Station, Danny One."

"What's a code of notes, Dr. Drago?"

"Still asking questions," he said amused. "Well, in a few seconds you won't be interested in silly things like that."

He pressed a button on the console, and I heard the soft hum of energy flowing through the computer and its wires.

"Close your eyes, Danny One," Otto Drago commanded.

I closed my eyes. Code of notes, I thought. What code?

"Otto Drago is your friend, Danny One," he said. What notes?

"Otto Drago will always look after you."

Codes usually meant numbers. I couldn't remember any numbers in his spaceship.

"Otto Drago will always love you."

All he did was punch the radio button and hum.

"You must stop asking him questions and always do what Otto Drago tells you to do. Repeat after me: 'I will always do what Otto Drago tells me to do.'"

"I will always do what Otto Drago tells me to do."

"I will sing the praises of Omega Station to other robots."

"I will sing the praises of Omega Station to other robots."

"I will tell them that robots do not need battery charges on Omega Station."

So that was why Ted Eight and Sally Five told Bob Three that.

"I will tell them that robots do not need battery charges on Omega Station."

By this time a real robot's computer pack would have surrendered to the reprogramming input. But through it all my mind kept returning to the puzzle of a code of notes.

"Repeat after me: 'When Otto Drago orders me, I will go into the deep pool of blue water.'"

"When Otto Drago orders me, I will go into the deep pool of blue water," I repeated.

I hadn't seen any notes in his spaceship. There weren't any letters. Any writing paper at all.

"And below the pool of blue water, in the glass cubicles, I will do the work that Otto Drago tells me to do."

What was this about? My mind spun between this new item and the code of notes.

"And below the pool of blue water, in the glass cubicles, I will do the work that Otto Drago tells me to do."

Concentrate on the notes. You can worry about the rest later. Only the code of notes can get Danny and the others inside.

"Otto Drago will direct me over a radio, and I will do what he bids without questions."

Maybe they were a different kind of notes.

"Otto Drago will direct me over a radio, and I will do what he bids without questions."

What kinds of notes were different? There were written notes, footnotes, pencil notes . . .

"Even though I may feel a little pain after a while, I will continue to work for Otto Drago . . ."

Notes . . . notes . . . notes . . . notes you write, notes you . . . you sing! Musical notes! My God, he had been humming a song while he punched the radio button on the flight console. He had punched the button to the rhythm of the song. What song had it been?

". . . because Otto Drago loves me."

". . . because Otto Drago loves me."

It had been a song I'd known. It had sounded familiar. A folk song. A song thousands of kids knew. A song thousands of kids had sung for thousands of years . . .

". . . and Otto Drago will look after me."

". . . and Otto Drago will look after me."

What was the name of that song?

"And when the universe finally explodes because of our great effort, to the others it will be an awesome shock . . ."

Shock!

". . . to the others it will be an awesome shock . . ."

It had something to do with *shock*. It rhymed with shock! That was it. The song. I remembered its name now. How could I have ever forgot?

"But to us it will be a great opportunity, for we will be masters of chaos, masters of debris . . ."

". . . masters of chaos, masters of debris . . ." I didn't know what he was talking about, I just repeated it, while my mind whirled. How was I to get the song title to Danny without Otto Drago knowing what I was doing?

"And then," said Otto Drago triumphantly, "we will stock the universe with Drago robots!"

"And then we will stock the universe with Drago robots!"

My mind raced along, looking for the right words.

"Beautiful," he said. "We are done. You may open your eyes, Danny One."

I opened my eyes. He began removing the electrodes from my wrists and forehead.

"How do you feel, Danny One?"

"Great," I lied.

He sat back and regarded me. His eyes were hard, appraising. The friendly stuff was over now. He didn't have to give me that phony smile anymore. I was now a robot programmed to love and adore him. Now I'd see the true Otto Drago in action.

He was going to test me now. I sensed that.

"Whom do you love, Danny One?" he asked.

"I love you"—I paused. I had an idea, an idea that might just save me, save the others—"like a *brother*."

"Good." He nodded. He liked my answer. I hoped Danny and the others did too. "And who will always look after you?" he asked.

I took a deep breath. You can do it, Jack Jameson, I said to myself. Take it easy.

"You will, Dr. Drago." I paused. I saw how to do it then. "Even if I feel a little pain after a while below the pool of blue water, even if I feel a *shock*, I know you will always look after me like a *brother*."

I'd emphasized those two words: *brother, shock*. Hear those two words, Danny, I prayed silently. Hear those two words!

"Good," Otto Drago snapped. "Now come along

[ 99 ]

with me, for it's time for you to take a swim in the Omega Station pool."

He wasn't asking me. He was commanding me.

I got up and walked to the door.

And forgot to walk stiff-in-the-knee.

He stared at me. My heart almost stopped. Our eyes met.

He closed the door. He took something out of his pocket. It was a laser pistol. He pointed it at me.

"Who are you?" he asked.

# 11  Cracking the Code

Later Danny told me that they had heard me empha-size the words *brother* and *shock*.

"He's trying to tell us something," Danny had said to the others.

"What?" Ann asked.

"Probably how to get inside Omega Station," Danny said.

"*Brother* and *shock*, Carl," Jeff said. "Quickly give us data on those words."

Carl went into his memory mode and started coming up with definitions of *brother*.

"A man or boy having the same parents. Fellow member of the same race, creed, profession, organi-zation. Those who are very close, work closely . . . like brothers."

That didn't seem to lead to anything.

"*Shock?*" Jeff asked.

"Shock," Carl said. "A sudden impact, collision, surprise . . ."

"Sudden impact," Jeff repeated. "Maybe we *are* supposed to blast our way into Omega Station."

"It couldn't mean that," Ann objected. "That would mean death for Jack, and it doesn't go with *brother.*"

"Maybe we're going about this the wrong way," Danny said.

"Maybe we are," Jeff snapped. "But right now Drago is probably taking Jack to the pool of water where the pain is."

They stared through the flight windows at the dark, ominous dome of Omega Station.

Jeff turned to Carl. "*Water*, Carl! What do you have on *water?*"

Danny told me later that he thought Jeff was really desperate when he asked that.

"Water," Carl repeated. He closed his eyes. His silicon chips were vibrating. "A colorless liquid, chemically a compound of hydrogen and oxygen, it is used for bathing, cleaning, drinking, fishing. It can be used as a shield, for steam, for swimming, temperature control, washing . . ."

He went on in alphabetical order. Every use of

water was familiar to them except water used as a "shield."

"How is water used as a shield?" Ann asked.

"Water has been used to protect humans from deadly radiation. As in the now obsolete nuclear reactors."

"Carl, what would deadly radiation do to an Atkins robot?" Jeff asked.

"For a while an Atkins robot would appear to be impervious to radiation, but after continued exposure at say ten thousand rems, an Atkins robot's meta-plastic skin would begin to crack. His or her insulation on the wires would crumble. There would be extreme metal fatigue in all his or her parts. Then he or she would begin to come apart."

"That's what happened to Bob Three," Danny said.

"And a human being, Carl? What would happen to a human being?" Ann asked.

"Ten thousand rems of radiation would kill a human instantly," Carl said.

"I bet anything," Jeff said slowly, because he was beginning to perceive what Otto Drago was up to, "that Drago has that pool of water to protect himself from radiation. He's making something very dangerous down there and is using robots to do the work."

"And," said Ann, frightened, "he thinks Jack is a robot who can enter the pool of water and do his awful work. He's probably sending Jack into the pool right now." She turned to Carl. Her voice was urgent. "Carl, we've got to figure out *brother shock*!"

Carl looked hurt. "Ann Two, my computer memory mode has already spoken on *brother shock*."

"What about the code of notes then?" Danny said. "What about *code*? Let's hear about *code*."

Carl closed his eyes with an air of resignation. "Code," he said. "Code: a body of laws, a set of principles, a set of signals, a system of secret writing."

"We know all that," Jeff said impatiently.

"Notes then," Ann said. "Tell us about notes."

"Notes can be short letters, memoranda, records of experience. Also there are notes as in tones of music of definite pitch, notes as in the keys of a piano or similar . . ."

"Music notes!" Ann cried out. "It could be a code of music notes!"

"You're right," Jeff said. He looked down at the radio button on the flight console. "Perhaps he pushed the radio button to a certain rhythm. That might have opened the dome. The rhythm might be the rhythm of a particular song. But what song?"

"It must have something to do with *brother shock*,"

Danny said. "Carl!"

"As I've told Ann Two already, Danny One. The computer has spoken on *brother shock*."

"Ask the computer to speak differently," Ann said. "Start with *brother*. What else does it know about *brother*? Anything about *brother*. Anything at all!"

Carl closed his eyes wearily. "Brother," he said. "In Chinese it is *di* or *ge*, depending on whether it is an older brother or younger. In Danish it is *broder*, in French it is *frere*, in German it is *bruder*, in Hebrew it is *ach,* in Italian it is *fratello*, in Spanish it is *hermano*, in Russian it is *brat*."

Ann quickly started pairing words.

"Di shock," she said. "Ge shock, broder shock, frere shock, bruder shock, ach shock, fratello shock, hermano shock, brat shock."

She looked at the others to see if any of the pairings made sense to them. They didn't.

Jeff turned to Danny. "You were programmed to be Jack's brother, weren't you?"

"Yes. And he's programmed to be my brother."

"Then maybe Jack's an important word too. Let's try *brother Jack*."

This time Ann paired all the different words for brother with Jack. "Di Jack, ge Jack, broder Jack, frere Jack, bruder . . ."

"One moment, everyone," Carl said. "I'm getting

feedback on . . . on frere Jack. Jack in French is Jacques. Pronounced in French correctly Jacques rhymes with *shock*."

There was a stunned silence.

" 'Frere Jacques,' " Danny said.

"Carl, hurry," Jeff said, "what do you have on 'Frere Jacques' ?"

"I'll go as fast as I can, Jeff," Carl said . . .

(If only Atkins robots had been programmed for old songs.)

Carl closed his eyes. " 'Frere Jacques,' " he began, "an old French children's song, approximately nine hundred years old. First sung in . . ."

"Forget its history," Jeff snapped. "How does the song go? The notes!"

"You know I can't sing, Jeff," Carl said. "I'm not programmed to keep a tune."

"For God's sake," Ann said, "just hum the notes."

Carl cleared his throat. "All right, but I'm not a very good hummer either."

Carl de dummed the song:

> da de dum dum
> da de dum dum
> dum dum dee
> dum dum dee
> dum dum dum de dum dum

> dum dum dum de dum dum
> dum de dum
> dum de dum

"Once more," Jeff said, his finger on the radio button.

And Carl sang his dum de dum dums once more.

And Jeff punched the button to the rhythm of the song.

And when they were done, Carl with his singing and Jeff with his button punching—the great dome of Omega Station slowly slid back.

And the C.O.L.A.R. spaceship quietly slipped in.

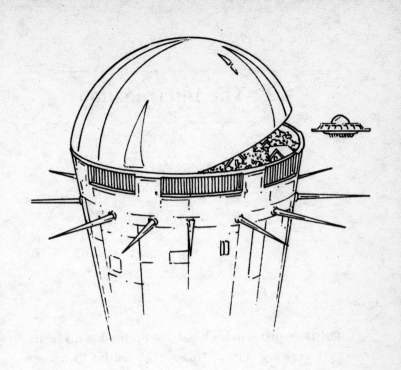

## 12 The Interrogation

The laser pistol in his hand was pointed at my heart.

"I repeat," Otto Drago said softly, "who are you?"

There was no point in lying anymore. He could easily find out the truth. Just cut me open. No wires or transistors. Just flesh and blood on his knife.

"My name is Jack Jameson . . ." I began. I had to find ways to stall, to give Danny and the others time to get inside Omega Station. ". . . and I'm a human being."

"Evidently," he sneered. He pointed to a straight-back chair along one wall. There were no electronic instruments near it.

"Sit in that chair there, Mister Jameson," he said.

If he was going to laser kill me in that chair, no

instruments would be damaged when I blew apart.

I sat down.

"Put your hands on your head, Mister Jameson."

I did that.

He sat down in a chair opposite me. "Now we will have a little talk without lies."

"Yes, sir," I said. I had to be polite, to try to get on his good side. If there was one.

"We will start on C.O.L.A.R., Mister Jameson. There you pretended to be a robot, did you not?"

He accented that "Mister" to show what contempt he had for humans.

"Yes, sir. I pretended to be a robot on C.O.L.A.R."

"Why?"

I paused. Tell the truth as much as possible. He is no dummy. Disarm him with politeness and truth.

"So I could be robotnapped by you, Dr. Drago."

"Why did you want to be robotnapped by me, Mister Jameson?"

"In order to find out what was happening to the missing robots of C.O.L.A.R."

"Hmmm . . ." He looked at me for a moment, guessing at things. "You're only about twelve years old. Surely you didn't think of this plan yourself. Who sent you?"

That had to come out sooner or later.

"Dr. Atkins."

Drago's face twisted in an angry grimace. "I thought as much. Leopold Atkins always gets in my way. He always tries to prevent me from accomplishing my work. I hate him. I . . ."

He stopped. He wasn't earning points getting angry in my presence. He looked at me. "How did Atkins know I was involved in these missing robots?"

"Bob Three was recovered."

"Ah . . . so that's it. And where did they find that scoundrel?"

"Floating near the Earth–Moon industrial highway."

He nodded. "Yes, that's about where he escaped. The scoundrel tricked me. I thought he had stopped functioning. I was going to place him in a cemetery orbit near Mars. But he escaped out a vent in my ship. Where is the traitor right now?"

I winced. The idea of that brave Bob Three being called a "traitor" was awful. Traitor to what? To whom?

"He . . . has stopped functioning."

"Good," Otto Drago said with pleasure. "He deserves to have died." He gave me a searching look. "But before he stopped functioning, I take it he told Leopold Atkins about me."

"Yes, sir."

"What exactly did he say?"

Oh, Danny, Ann, Jeff, Carl . . . hurry here. I can't keep this up too long.

I took a deep breath. "He said you were robot-napping Atkins robots. That Sally Five and Ted Eight were helping you. That Sam Ten and Barbara Two were here. He said there was blue water and pain. That's all he said."

"I didn't do a very complete job reprogramming that scoundrel," Otto Drago said. He looked at me. "Did Bob Three say what Atkins robots do here on Omega Station?"

"No, sir. What do they do?"

Otto Drago smiled. He was relaxing for the first time. He had nothing to fear from me, he realized. In fact, he could very easily and quickly dispose of me.

"They work here, Jack Jameson. As you will soon work here too. Though being a human being you won't do very well at the work. You won't last very long. Perhaps ten seconds at the most before you dissolve. An Atkins robot can last two weeks, which is one reason they are very precious to me. But you and I are mere humans, Mister Jameson, and therefore practically worthless."

"Are Ted Eight and Sally Five, Barbara Two and Sam Ten still here?"

"Yes. But they are worthless now. They've

cracked all over. I'll be putting them into a cemetery orbit any day now. That's why I went to C.O.L.A.R. To get robots to replace them. Unfortunately for you, you're not a robot."

"What's the work you want me to do?"

If I was going to die doing Otto Drago's work, even ten seconds of it, I at least wanted to know what that work was.

He chuckled. "Still playing the spy for Leopold. You know it was really very clever of him to send a human boy who could imitate a robot and not be reprogrammed. But then, there was never anything stupid about Leopold Atkins. He was and is a genius. I freely acknowledge that. But . . ." and here Otto Drago leaned forward, his eyes gleaming ". . . but so am I. And Leopold never gave me full credit. I worked with him to design the first robots. I shared the pain but not the triumph. And I adored our robots as much as he. But I saw their real uses and he never did. All Leopold wanted to do was create machines in the images of men and women, boys and girls, machines that would work with human beings and make life easier for them." Otto Drago snorted with contempt. "What I saw were machines that could take over the universe and under my direction create an orderly world: a world without emotions, without love or hate, without human beings. An efficient world!"

He's nuts, I thought. Absolutely nuts.

His eyes flashing, the laser pistol waving in his hand, Otto Drago rose to his feet.

"You ask what is our work here? Our work is to destroy in order to rebuild. To wipe clean in order to write new. To populate the Earth with Drago robots. That is our work. And that is why I had Omega Station towed to this side of the Moon. Where I could work in peace. And that is why I have recruited Atkins robots from C.O.L.A.R. And that . . ." he whispered to me "is why I am constructing the most beautiful weapons of terror that will wipe out that most terrible of all plagues— human beings!"

The laser gun waved dangerously under my nose.

"You want to know what we do here, Jack Jameson? Well, my young friend, you shall see with your own eyes, touch with your own hands, and fear with that fragile heart of yours. Up now. Up with you, human being pretending to be a robot. We shall see now what a good actor you are. We shall see you pretend in that most lovely of all places: the Omega Station swimming pool."

If there was one place I didn't want to see, it was that swimming pool. A place of pain for robots and instant death for humans.

"Up!" Otto Drago screamed at me when I didn't move.

I got up. And, without thinking, I picked up my green backpack and slung it over my shoulders. Back home Mom was always after me and Danny to pick up after ourselves. I hardly did it at all back home, but, for some reason, I did it here.

And then once more we were in the brilliant artificially lit world of Omega Station. My heart began to pound. I was a prisoner walking to my execution.

I looked up at the dome, outside of which the C.O.L.A.R. spaceship had to be, trying to figure out my message. If they didn't get inside soon, I would have to shout into my tooth radio: "Hum 'Frere Jacques' and punch the radio button to its rhythm." And then, of course, I would hardly get those words out of my mouth before Otto Drago would laser me apart.

Huge arc lights hung down from the dome. There were also light poles every twenty feet or so along the concrete paths. And from the poles, those emergency air helmets.

The paths went everywhere. Between trees, around bushes; they circled cottages, fountains. It looked like it might have been a pleasant place to live once.

It was now a bad place to die.

In one of those cottages Barbara Two and Sam

Ten, Sally Five and Ted Eight were probably dying right now.

I hesitated. I better try to stall some more.

"Which path do I take, sir?" I asked politely.

"All paths lead to the pool," Otto Drago said, and he poked me in the back with the laser gun. "Keep walking, Jack Jameson."

All paths eventually lead to the pool, and there the pool was, ahead of us: large, rectangular with white plastic sides. There was even a diving board at one end. And metal ladders at the other end.

And bordering the pool, beautiful maple trees. It really could be a summer camp. And a reprogrammed robot might think that was just where he was.

We passed more light poles with air helmets hanging from them, and then we approached the swimming pool. Why was a swimming pool so dangerous? What was the work they did in it, or under it?

I knew I'd soon find out, and my knees began to shake. I didn't want to find out.

Once more I looked up at the dome. Why didn't they make it slide back?

I'd have to shout the code out, and that would be the end of me.

We came up to the pool's edge. The water was

blue and clear. It looked lovely. Like a dream place to swim.

I stopped.

"Keep moving, Mister Jameson," Otto Drago said behind me. "I want you to see the bottom."

I stepped up onto the edge and looked down to the bottom.

I gasped.

There on the bottom were six long silver fish.

Each fish lay suspended in a glass cubicle.

Each fish had a long sharp nose and a torpedo-like tail.

No . . . one of the fish had no nose.

Otto Drago looked down too. His eyes glistened. "Aren't they beautiful?" he murmured.

"Yes, sir," I gulped. "But what are they?"

"Old-fashioned weapons. Leftovers from another century. And discovered by me in a cave on the dark side of the Moon. I brought them here. They are the last nuclear bombs in the universe, outlawed by mankind, but now being rearmed with plutonium by me. Only one is left to be armed. And its plutonium charge is in the cubicle with it. Arming the last bomb is your task, Jack Jameson."

He smiled at me.

"You, my young friend, are going to dive into the pool and enter the last watertight cubicle. I will direct you by radio in the cubicle on how to arm this last bomb."

So that's what it was all about. An amusingly cruel way of killing me. He'd already told me that human beings couldn't last ten seconds in the water. If it was plutonium, then the water was a killer liquid. A robot could live in it for a few days and be OK, but even repeated exposure for a robot would destroy it. I remembered how Bob Three had looked.

The laser pistol was aimed at my head.

Now was the time to shout out to Danny, I thought. To yell: " 'Frere Jacques' . . . from Brother Jack to Brother Danny"—one last good-bye.

"Into the water with you, Jack Jameson," Otto Drago said. "And if you do the job for me, I will free you."

I tried stalling one last time. "If I can arm the last nuclear bomb for you before I die, will you make sure my folks who live in Region III, U.S.A., don't get hurt?"

"Of course," he lied. "Now into the pool!"

I closed my eyes. My plan was to count to three and then yell: " 'Frere Jacques' ! Punch the button!"

By then I'd be dead.

"Jump in," he ordered.

One, I counted to myself.

Two . . .

His forefinger showed white as it tightened on the trigger of the laser pistol.

Good-bye, dear world, I thought. Good-bye fishing and trees, good-bye to everyone.

I took a deep breath and was about to shout " 'Frere Jacques' " to Danny when the world I'd been saying good-bye to suddenly said good-bye to me.

It disappeared.

The lights went out all over Omega Station.

"What the devil," Otto Drago exclaimed.

I ran for it.

# 13  The Big Switch

The "it" I ran for was the nearest emergency air helmet. I heard Otto Drago scream that a generator had failed, and he must have been running for an emergency air helmet too.

And then, I hoped, he'd be running to the air generators to see why they had failed.

I was positive it wasn't a power failure in Omega Station. What had happened, or what I hoped had happened, was that the C.O.L.A.R. spaceship had finally entered Omega Station and the dome was swinging back, cutting out the lights.

It wasn't easy finding an air helmet in the dark. I ran holding my breath because when I let it out, there'd be no more air to breathe.

I finally ran smack into a light pole and groped in

the dark till my hands came in contact with an air helmet. I stuck it over my head, and in a second I had the air system working. I was now breathing off the helmet's air supply.

Everyone practices doing this in the space colonies.

I looked up. Overhead it was a different scene. White dots in a black sky blinked at me. Stars. I was right. The dome had swung back, and the C.O.L.A.R. spaceship was now in. In a little while Otto Drago would put two and two together, realizing it wasn't the generators. But my hope now was that he was somewhere below tinkering with a machine.

Quickly my eyes grew accustomed to the darkness. The starlight helped. I picked out the small, neat cottages, the trees, the fountains . . . and then, far off, I spotted a dark shape moving slowly, cautiously toward the center of Omega Station.

That had to be the C.O.L.A.R. spaceship. I ran toward it. And as I ran, a plan formed itself in my mind. Dr. Atkins had planned for us to make a big switch on Otto Drago, but he didn't know exactly how we could stop the evil man. I thought of a way to take care of Drago without blowing us all up. Because those nuclear weapons were dangerous.

As I ran the backpack bounced on my shoulders, with the key items inside.

We'd have to move fast if my plan was to work. Drago would soon enough discover what had caused the power "failure."

The dark shape moving slowly *was* the C.O.L.A.R. spaceship. I couldn't see anyone inside it. It was too dark for that.

Radio contact them, I thought. And don't let any of them except Danny come out.

I slapped my tongue against my back tooth.

"Danny, this is Jack. Can you hear me?"

Danny answered immediately. "Jack. Where are you? Are you OK?"

"I'm fine. I'm right outside the ship . . ."

"We're coming out," Jeff said.

"No. Just Danny. The rest of you guys have got to leave. I'll call you back. Listen, Drago's dangerous. He's got six nuclear bombs with plutonium warheads that he could explode any second. I've got a plan to get rid of him and save the other robots. They're barely alive in one of the cottages here."

"What's your plan? And where's Drago now?"

"He thinks a generator has broken down and is checking it out . . ." There was really no time to tell them my plan, but I knew they wouldn't leave me unless I did, so I told them the plan I'd formed while running.

"That's crazy," Ann said. "It'll never work."

"Percentage of success, Carl?" Jeff snapped.

"Nineteen percent," Carl replied.

"That's terrible," Ann said.

"No, it's great," I said. "I need Danny for it. I . . ."

But Danny was already coming out the door and down the ramp. I grabbed his hand.

"You guys get out of here with the ship. Play 'Frere Jacques' again once you're out and the dome'll close. Hurry! Danny, you come with me."

"Where to, Jack?"

"The swimming pool where Drago last saw me."

The C.O.L.A.R. spaceship reversed engines and was moving quickly off. In seconds it would be gone, and the dome would close and the lights would go on again, and the air would be contained again.

Danny and I ran together in the darkness back to the swimming pool. There was no sign of Otto Drago, which meant he was still busy in the generator room, wherever that was. As we passed a light pole, I grabbed another emergency helmet and gave it to Danny.

"Put it on."

"I'm a robot, I don't need it."

"You'll need it if you're going to be me. And put this on too."

I shifted the backpack from me to him. Then I watched him as he adjusted his air helmet. It was funny to see an Atkins robot who didn't need to wear an air helmet now wearing one.

"Listen," I said, "the big thing now is not to move much. Don't walk or he'll spot the stiff-in-the-knee. Just stand on the edge of the pool. And you remember what you're supposed to do?"

"I remember, Jack. Where are you going to be?"

I looked around. One of the maple trees was nearby. It was in full leaf. I could climb that and hide pretty good up there.

"Up there watching you."

"Don't make any noise up there."

"I won't. Here we are. This is the pool."

"It doesn't look so bad."

"It is. Wait till the lights go on and you see the bombs down there. Good luck, Danny. Don't stay in the water any longer than you have to."

Danny grinned. "I won't. And you—don't fall out of that tree and embarrass me."

We both laughed. It was crazy. Laughing like that at a time like this. But that's what it's like when your robot buddy and you go into action. Nothing can stop us. I hope.

Although it was dark, I went up that tree pretty fast. Which was a good thing because no sooner had

I got settled behind some fat maple leaves than the lights went on again in Omega Station.

From my perch, I looked down on Danny. He was peering over the side of the pool at the six nuclear bombs.

"I see them, Jack," he whispered to me over his radio.

"Be careful you don't fall in," I whispered to him.

I heard a noise in the distance.

"Drago's coming," I whispered. "Be careful."

Through the leaves of the tree, I saw Otto Drago hurrying down a path toward the swimming pool. He had the laser pistol in his hand. And he was still wearing an emergency air helmet.

He looked worried, but when he caught sight of Danny standing there, he smiled. He removed his air helmet.

"Well, Jack Jameson," he said, "you knew how to save yourself, didn't you? You can take off your helmet now. The power is back on. It must have been a temporary malfunction in a generator."

Danny took off the helmet he hadn't needed in the first place. Up in the tree, I took mine off too.

Drago beamed at Danny. "I saw you run for the helmet. Very sensible of you, and even more sensible of you to return here. You understood, of

course, that there was no escape from Omega Station."

"I knew that," Danny said politely.

"Good. I can see we two will get along. Now for a little work on one of my beautiful nuclear bombs."

"Yes, sir," Danny said, and then he hesitated.

"Sneeze," I whispered to him over my radio.

"I'm ready to go into the pool and . . . and . . . uh . . . uh . . . hachoo!"

Danny gave one of the great sneezes of all time.

"Oh, boy, I'm getting . . ." He sneezed again, and again ". . . sick," he said.

"Don't worry," Otto Drago assured him, smiling evilly, "the swimming pool will cure you of your sickness."

"Oh, I've got something better than that," Danny said. "I've got an Alpha pill. That prevents all sickness."

"A what pill?" Drago asked.

"An Alpha pill," Danny said. "It's a new kind of pill to protect humans. It makes them as strong as robots in preventing all kinds of sickness and disease. Dr. Atkins invented them. Nothing can hurt me if I take an Alpha pill."

Otto Drago was amused. "An Alpha pill, is it? Well, what better place to take one of your Alpha pills than on Omega Station. By the way, do you know what Omega stands for, my little human friend?"

"No, sir," Danny said, taking out the little box of hay fever pills my mother had insisted on my taking on the mission.

"Omega stands for the end. I am the alpha and the omega, the beginning and the end." Drago chuckled. "You may have the beginning in those little pills, Jack Jameson, but I have the end down there. All right, Jack, take your little pill and get into the water."

Danny swallowed the hay fever pill he didn't need. Otto Drago watched him much amused. Then Danny put the box of pills inside the backpack. He was following the plan perfectly.

"All right. No more excuses," Drago snapped. "Into the pool. And this time there will be no lights going out."

"Go in slowly," I whispered to Danny.

"I will," Danny said, answering me.

"You will what?" Otto Drago asked Danny.

Oh, Danny, I thought, with a sinking feeling.

"I will hope that this time the lights don't go out, so I can arm your beautiful nuclear weapons," Danny said.

Drago beamed. "Good."

Good? That was a *great* recovery!

"Now . . . enter the pool."

Slowly Danny let himself into the beautiful blue but deadly swimming pool. Otto Drago, smiling, looked at his watch. He was going to measure off the ten seconds before the human being he had forced into the water dissolved to nothingness.

The big switch was on.

And now we had to see if it would work.

# 14 Red Dot in a Blue Pool

Ten . . . nine . . . eight . . . seven . . . six . . .

Otto Drago glanced from his watch to the pool to his watch to the pool . . .

I saw it all happen from my perch in the maple tree.

Danny dove down to the bottom of the pool and swam around there looking into the glass cubicles.

. . . five . . . four . . .

Otto Drago watched expectantly for Danny to begin to break up and dissolve. But Danny just swam leisurely around the cubicles, until he finally opened one, entered the air lock, opened the inner door and went inside.

Now he was in practically direct contact with the deadly plutonium radiation.

. . . three . . . two . . .

Drago held his breath. (So did I.)

Then Danny left the cubicle and swam easily up to the surface where he treaded water and smiled up at Drago.

. . . one . . . zero . . .

Drago's mouth was open in amazement.

"Jack Jameson," he stammered, "are . . . are you . . . all . . . right?"

He glanced at his watch. Perhaps his watch was off. This human boy should have dissolved into nothingness already.

"Hey, I'm fine," Danny said cheerfully. "Now what exactly do you want me to do down there?"

"But . . . but . . . but . . . I don't understand this at all. You should have been dissolved. It's over . . . over thirty seconds already."

"Dissolved?" Danny laughed. "Man, I never felt better in my life. Those Alpha pills chase away all sickness. Hey, Dr. Drago, you said you'd let me go free if I worked for you, didn't you?"

"Yes . . . but . . . but . . . that is plutoniumated water. There are more than one hundred thousand rems of radiation there. It's . . . impossible."

I slapped my rear tooth with my tongue to make sure my radio was still on.

"Tell him that Alpha pills protect humans against everything, especially radiation," I whispered.

"Alpha pills protect humans against everything, especially radiation," Danny said. It was just the reverse of him giving me the conveyance answer back on C.O.L.A.R. this morning.

Otto Drago shook his head in amazement. He looked at his watch. "Over two minutes and you are still in the plutonium water. And you are still alive. And well." He looked at Danny. "Tell me, Jack, do you feel any pain at all?"

"Not a smidgin," Danny said, and to prove it he swam a brisk backstroke across the pool.

[ 134 ]

"What about your muscles?" Drago called out. "Do you ache there?"

"Nope," said Danny, and to prove it he flipped head over heels in the water and did an Australian crawl back to where Drago was standing.

"What about your head? Do you have a head-ache?"

"My head's clear. I'm thinking very clearly," Danny said.

Easy, Danny, I thought. Don't get cute.

Drago leaned forward.

"Seven times seven?" he asked.

"Forty-nine," Danny said.

"What's the largest animal on Earth?"

"The great blue whale."

"The capital of Australia is?"

"Canberra."

"Amazing," Drago said. He stared down at my green backpack. "It must be the Alpha pill," he murmured. "What else could it be?"

He picked up my backpack and took out my little jar of hay fever pills. He held the pills up, and suddenly he began to laugh. It was crazy laughter that echoed insanely around the emptiness of Omega Station.

He shouted out to no one: "In my hands the alpha. Below is the omega. I have both the alpha and the omega in my power."

Then he thought of something and looked down again at Danny.

"Jack," he said, "tell me exactly: how long do these pills protect a human being?"

"Six hours," I whispered.

"Six hours," Danny said.

"Six hours," Otto Drago repeated, and once again the crazy laughter emerged from his mouth.

"It took God six days to create the world," he shouted out into the great dome, "but I, Otto Drago, can destroy it in six hours. Don't you see what this means, Jack Jameson? I don't need you or anyone else to arm my last nuclear warhead. I can do it myself. Ha, Leopold Atkins! You thought that a human boy armed with Alpha pills could conquer me, but little did you know that I would end up with his Alpha pills."

He took the cover off the jar of pills.

"Pills of life," he chanted, "bombs of death. You both belong to me!"

And then with a mighty gulp he swallowed all the hay fever pills at once.

And threw away the empty jar and raised his hands high in the air.

"I am the alpha and the omega, the beginning and the end. It is I who will bring death to the

[ 136 ]

universe, so I can rebuild it in my image. I, Otto Drago, am the new God!"

And then with a mighty jump, Otto Drago, the new God, leaped into the blue water and dove eagerly to the bottom.

I jumped down from my perch in the tree. Danny climbed out of the pool and together we stood on the edge and watched Otto Drago swim down to the door of the last cubicle, where the final nuclear bomb was waiting to be armed.

". . . ten . . . nine . . . eight," *I* began the count this time.

Drago opened the glass door and entered the air lock.

He went through the inner door.

". . . seven . . . six . . . five . . ."

He put his hands tenderly on the long deadly nuclear fish . . .

". . . four . . . three . . . two . . ."

At that moment Drago must have sensed something wrong. He turned and looked up, looked through the clear glass, the clear blue water at us. At me and Danny, the two of us, twins, brown hair, freckles, look alikes, staring down at him in the water.

He stared and stared, and then you could see him realizing what had happened. A strange look came over his face.

He burst out of the glass cubicle. He was swimming hard . . . trying to get to the surface as fast as he could.

". . . one . . . zero," I said.

Drago didn't make it.

Even as we watched his face was turning red, bright beet red, and then his whole body was turning red. At the same time he was getting smaller, shrinking from the feet up like a thin red line in the water, until all that was left was his face, a bright red face with the comical features and the big ears . . .

And then his face too began to shrink, got smaller and smaller, until all that was left was a dot in the water.

A red dot in the blue water.

And then the red dot too was gone, and the deadly blue water lapped silently against the edges of the pool. The most dangerous swimming pool in the universe.

I don't know how long Danny and I stood there, staring at what had just happened, not saying a word to each other . . . Finally it was a voice coming out of Danny's belly button and echoing inside my head that woke us both up.

"C.O.L.A.R. spaceship to Jack and Danny Jameson," Jeff was calling, "are you guys OK? What's going on inside there?"

We looked at each other.

"You tell him," we both said at once.

"Tell us what?" Ann's voice came on.

"Otto Drago's dissolved," I said.

"What?" Jeff asked, incredulously.

"That's right," Danny said, "Drago has dissolved."

"To dissolve," we heard Carl's voice, "means to make or become liquid, to melt, to break up, to disintegrate, to end."

Drago was the omega himself—the end, I thought. And Danny, my robot buddy, was the alpha—the beginning.

"We're coming back in," Jeff said. "I want to see if you guys are OK or not."

# 15 End of an Adventure

We were OK, but it dawned on us that maybe there were others on Omega Station who were not.

So as soon as we got through telling Jeff, Ann, and Carl what had happened to Drago, and they too had stared at the blue water and the dangerous silver "fish" at the bottom, we all began a cottage by cottage search for the missing robots.

We found them, one to a cottage, lying on beds, staring lifelessly at the ceilings, waiting for Otto Drago to collect them and put them in cemetery orbits.

Ted Eight was the first one we found.

"Ted," Jeff said, "it's Jeff. From C.O.L.A.R. Everything's going to be all right now."

"Welcome to Omega Station, Jeff," Ted Eight

replied tonelessly. "This is a wonderful place, Jeff. If you do what Dr. Drago tells you to do, Jeff, you will be happy here and never need a battery charge."

"We've got to reprogram him right away," Ann said.

"First, we've got to get his body fixed up," Jeff said.

"Both can be done at Dr. Atkins's factory," Danny said.

"What about the bombs here on Omega Station?" I asked.

Jeff nodded. "Jack's right. Before we leave we have to disarm those bombs. A meteorite could crash into this place and the whole Earth system would be contaminated for years to come."

Carl punched up his computer data mode on disarming nuclear weapons and then he and Jeff dove into the pool and disarmed the five plutonium bombs.

After that we carried the four sick robots (none of whom were as badly off as Bob Three had been) into the C.O.L.A.R. spaceship, and Jeff and Carl flew them to Earth and to the Atkins Factory.

Danny, Ann, and I followed in the red-and-black Omega Station ship.

Jeff radioed ahead and told Dr. Atkins everything that had happened on Omega Station. Dr. Atkins had his entire emergency repair crew waiting for them at the spaceport on the roof of the factory. They took the four sick robots down to emergency repair right away.

The rest of us waited anxiously in Dr. Atkins's office. Finally after what seemed like an eternity, Dr. Atkins came in. He looked tired but he was smiling.

"They're all going to be all right. Otto Drago didn't work them in the pool as hard as he had Bob Three. Apparently he didn't like Bob Three, so he gave him ten times the amount of time in the pool. The pain was also what may have let Bob Three's reprogramming wear off before Drago was ready to dump him. And that led him to escape. In a little while the others will be off to reprogramming, and their Omega Station experience will be just a bad memory. And that too, in time, will disappear."

"That's fine," Jeff said.

"If only Bob Three could be here too," Ann said wistfully.

"I think that can be arranged," Dr. Atkins said. He punched a button on his Vue/Phone. "Send him in," he ordered.

A moment later, to our complete amazement, Bob Three walked into Dr. Atkins's office. He was grinning from ear to ear.

"I don't believe this," Jeff said.

"Hello, Jeff," Bob Three said. "Hello, Ann, Carl, Jack, and Danny."

"You're not Bob Three," Jeff said. "Who are you?"

Bob Three laughed. "No, I'm not really Bob Three. I guess you could say I'm Bob Three and One-Half. They just finished creating me this morning. Dr. Atkins designed me to look exactly like a robot named Bob Three and programmed me to be just like him. So, in a way, I am him. Don't you think that Dr. Atkins did a great job?"

"Yes," Ann said, "but it is a little creepy."

"Thank you," Dr. Atkins said. "I'll accept that as a compliment in this case. Bob Three will live on in Bob Three and One-Half."

"I think we'll call you 'Halfy' for short," Ann said.

"Good," Bob Three and One-Half said.

"As for Omega Station," Dr. Atkins went on, "I intend to have it towed to the bright side of the Moon. The weapons will be completely demolished. The swimming pool will be replaced with clean and healthy water, and Omega Station will become just what Otto Drago pretended it was—a summer camp!"

What a cheer went up from all of us!

Dr. Atkins acknowledged the cheer with a modest bow.

"Now," he said, "I would like to salute the real heroes of this adventure: Jack and Danny Jameson. They have, today, saved the life of the whole universe."

I blushed, and Danny, who was programmed to blush, blushed too.

"Speech!" Ann said. "The heroes have to make speeches."

"No, thanks," I said. "I'm no good at speeches."

"Neither am I," Danny said, grinning. "Besides, the person who really saved the universe isn't even here."

"Who's that?" they all asked.

"Jack's mom," Danny said. "She was the one who made him take hay fever pills on the mission."

There was a silence. "By God, Danny One is right," Dr. Atkins said. "Mrs. Jameson is the real hero. And you two better get home right away. Your folks are probably worried about you."

And so after quick good-byes to Jeff, Ann, Carl, and Bob Three and One-Half, and a promise from us to visit C.O.L.A.R. during Christmas vacation, I returned the tooth radio to Dr. Atkins, who said I wouldn't need it . . ."for a while."

Then Danny and I flew home in the same Atkins Factory cruiser that picked us up yesterday after school. The pilot dropped us off at our house near the corner of Dexter and Church roads in Region III.

As we ran up the drive to our house, we could see Mom and Dad at the supper table. We opened the door and ran in.

Dad let out a whoop and grabbed us both in his big arms.

"The boys are back," he chortled.

Mom hugged us hard too. But then she frowned. "Jack, your backpack? Did you leave it somewhere?"

"Gosh. I must have left it at Omega Station."

"Omega Station?" Dad said. "What's that?"

"It's a faraway place," Danny said.

"Did you at least remember to take your hay fever pills while you were gone?" Mom asked me.

"No. But Danny took one," I said, grinning.

"And Otto Drago took all the rest," Danny said, laughing.

"He must have been a very sick man," Mom said.

"He *was*," we said together.

"Maybe you better sit down and tell us what happened to you both," Dad said.

And so we told them. From the beginning. Getting my tooth radio in Dr. Atkins's office, the trip to C.O.L.A.R., getting robotnapped by Otto Drago, the trip to Omega Station, Danny and the others following us, the 'Frere Jacques' code, the swimming pool, the bombs, and the hay fever pills that saved the life of the universe.

When we were done, Mom and Dad sat there in a shocked silence.

Finally Mom said: "Why, you were in terrible danger, both of you."

And Dad said: "I think you both better stay close to home for a while."

"We will," Danny assured them. "We were going to play basketball yesterday when . . ."

He didn't finish his sentence. Just then his bellybutton radio went off again. We couldn't believe it. We stared at each other.

"Let's not answer it, Jack," Danny said.

I took a deep breath. "Let's, Danny," I said.

And, of course, we did.

But that's another story.